I squeezed back into the tree and slipped my two
sharpest blades into the scabbards on my chest.
Then I pulled on my long, thick, black overcoat,
which has thirteen buttons made of best-quality
bone. The coat comes down as far as my brown
leather boots and the sleeves are long enough to
cover my hairy arms.

I'm hairy all over – and there's something else
I should mention. Something that makes me
different from you.

I have a tail.

Don't laugh – don't pull a face or shake your head.
Be sensible and feel sorry for yourself because you
don't have one. You see, mine's a long, powerful
tail that's better than an extra arm.

One more thing – my name is Slither, and before
my tale is finished you'll find out why.

THE WARDSTONE CHRONICLES

BOOK ONE:
THE SPOOK'S APPRENTICE

BOOK TWO:
THE SPOOK'S CURSE

BOOK THREE:
THE SPOOK'S SECRET

BOOK FOUR:
THE SPOOK'S BATTLE

BOOK FIVE:
THE SPOOK'S MISTAKE

BOOK SIX:
THE SPOOK'S SACRIFICE

BOOK SEVEN:
THE SPOOK'S NIGHTMARE

BOOK EIGHT:
THE SPOOK'S DESTINY

BOOK NINE:
SPOOK'S: I AM GRIMALKIN

BOOK TEN:
THE SPOOK'S BLOOD

BOOK ELEVEN:
SPOOK'S: SLITHER'S TALE

ALSO AVAILABLE

THE SPOOK'S STORIES:
WITCHES

THE SPOOK'S BESTIARY

Illustration by Julek Heller called 'Kobalos'

EXTRACT FROM THE SPOOKS BESTIARY

Illustrated by Julek Heller

The Kobalos

The Kobalos are not human. They walk upright but have something of the appearance of a fox or a wolf. The body is covered with dark hair; the face and hands are shaven according to custom; the mage wears a long black coat with a slit in the back to accommodate his tail, which can function as an extra limb.

These mages are solitary creatures who shun their fellow citizens and usually dwell beyond the fringes of the frozen Kobalos domain, which is far to the north of the continent known as Europa. Each one 'farms' a haizda, a territory which he has marked out as his own. Within it there are several hundred humans, living in hamlets, villages and farms. He rules by fear and magecraft, harvesting souls and accumulating power. He usually lives in an old, gnarled ghanbala tree, sleeping by day but travelling the boundaries of his haizda by night, taking the blood of humans and animals for sustenance. He can shift his shape, taking on the appearance of animals, and can also vary his size. This type of mage is also a formidable warrior whose favourite weapon is a sabre.

The Kobalos are a fierce, warlike race who, with the exception of their mages, inhabit Valkarky, a city deep within the Arctic Circle.

The name Valkarky means the City of the Petrified Tree; it is filled with all types of abomination that have been created by dark magic. Its walls are constructed and renewed by creatures that never sleep; creatures that spit soft stone from their mouths. The Kobalos believe that their city will not stop growing until it covers the entire world.*

*The above is based upon the writings of a very early spook called Nicholas Browne, who travelled far beyond the borders of the County. Apart from his notebooks, there is no evidence that any of his assertions are true but we must keep an open mind. The world is a big place and much remains to be explored – John Gregory

SPOOK'S
SLITHER'S TALE

JOSEPH DELANEY

Interior illustrations by David Wyatt

THE BODLEY HEAD
London

SPOOK'S: SLITHER'S TALE

A BODLEY HEAD BOOK
Hardback: 978 0 370 33217 8
Trade Paperback: 978 0 370 33218 5

Published in Great Britain by The Bodley Head,
an imprint of Random House Children's Publishers UK
A Random House Group Company

This edition published 2012

1 3 5 7 9 10 8 6 4 2

Text copyright © Joseph Delaney, 2012
Cover illustration copyright © Talexi Taini, 2012
Interior illustrations copyright © David Wyatt, 2012

The right of Joseph Delaney to be identified as the author of this work has been
asserted in accordance with the Copyright, Designs and Patents Act 1988.

The Random House Group Limited supports the Forest Stewardship Council (FSC®), the leading
international forest certification organization. Our books carrying the FSC label are printed on
FSC®-certified paper. FSC is the only forest certification scheme endorsed by the leading
environmental organizations, including Greenpeace. Our paper procurement policy can
be found at www.randomhouse.co.uk/environment.

MIX
Paper from
responsible sources
FSC® C016897

Set in 10.5/16.5 Palatino by Falcon Oast Graphic Art Ltd

RANDOM HOUSE CHILDREN'S PUBLISHERS UK
61–63 Uxbridge Road, London W5 5SA

www.randomhousechildrens.co.uk
www.totallyrandombooks.co.uk
www.randomhouse.co.uk

Addresses for companies within The Random House Group Limited can be
found at: www.randomhouse.co.uk/offices.htm

THE RANDOM HOUSE GROUP Limited Reg. No. 954009

A CIP catalogue record for this book is available from the British Library.

Printed and bound in Great Britain by Clays Ltd, St Ives plc for Marie

FAR FROM THE WARDSTONE . . .

Back in the County, things have rarely looked more dangerous for Tom Ward. His master the Spook has been weakened by years of battle, his closest friend Alice has disappeared on a dangerous quest, and Tom may now be the only one who can prevent the Fiend from returning to bring new terror to the world.

But while his battle wages on, the dark never rests – in the County or elsewhere. And far to the north, a long way from Tom's lands, a new darkness is rising.

This book takes place shortly after the events of *The Spook's Blood*, and it tells of new creatures, new lands, and new horrors beyond imagination . . .

This is *Slither's Tale*.

THE HIGHEST POINT IN THE COUNTY
IS MARKED BY MYSTERY.
IT IS SAID THAT A MAN DIED THERE IN A
GREAT STORM, WHILE BINDING AN EVIL
THAT THREATENED THE WHOLE WORLD.
THEN THE ICE CAME AGAIN, AND WHEN IT
RETREATED, EVEN THE SHAPES OF THE
HILLS AND THE NAMES OF THE TOWNS
IN THE VALLEYS CHANGED.
NOW, AT THAT HIGHEST POINT ON
THE FELLS, NO TRACE REMAINS OF WHAT
WAS DONE SO LONG AGO,
BUT ITS NAME HAS ENDURED.
THEY CALL IT –

THE WARDSTONE.

PROLOGUE
NESSA'S NIGHTMARE

I t is very dark in my bedroom. The candle has guttered, the flame has flickered and died. It is cold too, despite the extra blankets. It has been a long winter, one of the very worst. This is spring but there is still a crust of frozen snow on the fields and the farmyard flags, and also ice inside my room patterning the windowpanes.

But it is my birthday tomorrow. I will be ten. I am looking forward to the cake. I have to blow out all its candles with one really big breath. If I do that, Father will give me my present. It is a dress – a red dress with white lace at the neck and hem.

I want to sleep. I squeeze my eyes tight shut and try. It's

better to sleep because then the night will pass quickly. I will open my eyes to see sunlight streaming in through the window, dust motes gleaming like tiny suns.

Suddenly I hear a noise. What is it? It sounds like something scratching on the floor by the wainscot. Could it be a rat? I fear big grey rats with their small eyes and long whiskers. My greatest fear of all is that one might find its way into my bed.

My heart begins to race with fear and I think of calling out for my father. But my mother died two years ago and he manages the farm all by himself. His days are long and tiring and he needs his sleep. No, I must be brave. The rat will soon go away. Why should it bother with my bed? There is no food here.

Again there comes a scratching of sharp claws on wood. My heart jumps with fear. The noise is nearer now, halfway between the window and my bed. I hold my breath, listening for the sound to be repeated. It is, and now it is much closer, just below my bed. If I were to look down, it might be staring up at me with its small beady eyes.

I *must* get up. I will run to my father's room. But what if the rat's whiskers touch my feet? What if I tread on its long thin tail?

Now it gets even louder. I feel a tug at my bedclothes and shiver with fear. The rat is climbing up onto my bed, using its claws to pull itself on top of the blankets. In a panic I try to sit up. But I can't. I seem to be paralysed. I can open my mouth, but when I scream, no sound escapes my lips.

The rat is crawling up onto my body now. I can feel its small sharp claws pricking into my skin through the blankets. It is sitting on my chest. Its tail goes *thumpety-thump*, faster and faster, keeping perfect time with the beating of my heart.

And now there is a new thing, even more terrifying. The rat seems to be growing heavier by the second. Its weight is pressing down on my chest, making it difficult to breathe. How can that be possible? How can a rat be so large and heavy?

Now, in the darkness, I sense its face moving closer to mine. It's a big face and I can feel the rat's warm breath on my skin. But there is something even stranger than its size and weight. Its eyes are glowing in the dark. They are large and red, and by their lurid glare I can now see its face.

It isn't a rat, after all. The face is that of a fox or wolf, with a long jaw and big sharp teeth. And those teeth are biting into my neck now. Long, thin, hot needles of pain pierce my throat.

I scream. Over and over again, I scream silently. I feel as if I am dying, slipping down into the deepest darkness, away from this world.

Then I am awake and the weight is gone from my chest. I can move now, and I sit up in bed and begin to cry. Soon I hear the sound of heavy boots pounding across the wooden boards of the corridor. The door is flung open, and Father enters carrying a candle.

He places it on the bedside table, and moments later I am

in his arms. I sob and sob, and he strokes my hair and pats my back in reassurance.

'It's all right. It's all right, daughter,' he murmurs. 'It was just a dream – just a terrible nightmare.'

But then he holds me at arm's length and studies my face, neck and shoulders carefully. Next he takes a white handkerchief from the pocket of his nightshirt and gently dabs it at my neck. He scrunches it up in his hand and quickly thrusts it back into his pocket. But not quite fast enough to prevent me from seeing the spots of blood.

Is the nightmare over?

Am I awake?

Or am I still dreaming?

CHAPTER 1
IS IT A TRADE?

I woke up feeling very thirsty.

I'm always thirsty when I wake up, so there was nothing different there, no hint at all that this would be a day to remember.

I climbed out through the cleft, high in the trunk of my old ghanbala tree, and gazed down upon the white, frosty ground far below.

The sun wouldn't rise fully for almost an hour and the stars were still visible. I knew all five thousand of them by name, but Cougis, the Dog Star, was my favourite. It was red, a bloodshot eye peering through the black velvet curtain that the Lord of Night casts over the sky.

I had been asleep for almost three months. I always sleep through that time – the darkest, coldest part of winter, which we call *shudru*. Now I was awake, and thirsty.

It was too close to dawn for taking blood from the humans in my haizda – the ones I farmed. My next preference would be to hunt, but nothing would be about yet. There was nothing to satisfy my thirst – yet there was another way. I could always go and intimidate Old Rowler and force him to trade.

I squeezed back into the tree and slipped my two sharpest blades into the scabbards on my chest. Then I pulled on my long, thick, black overcoat, which has thirteen buttons made of best-quality bone. The coat comes down as far as my brown leather boots and the sleeves are long enough to cover my hairy arms.

I'm hairy all over – and there's something else I should mention. Something that makes me different from you.

I have a tail.

Don't laugh – don't pull a face or shake your head. Be sensible and feel sorry for yourself because you don't have one. You see, mine's a long, powerful tail that's better than an extra arm.

One more thing – my name is Slither, and before my tale is finished you'll find out why.

Finally I laced up my boots and squeezed back through the cleft and onto the branch.

Then I stepped out into space.

I counted to two before flicking up my slithery tail. It coiled and tightened; the skin rasped against the lowest branch, breaking off shards of bark that fell like dark flakes of snow. I hung there by my tail for a few seconds while my keen eyes searched the ground below. There were no tracks to mark the frost. Not that I expected any. My ears are sharp and I awake at the slightest sound, but it's always better to be safe than sorry.

I dropped again, landing on the cold hard ground. Then I began to run, watching the ground speed by in a blur beneath my legs. Within minutes I'd be at Old Rowler's farm.

I respected Old Rowler.

I respected him just enough to turn what might have been a cruel taking into a wary trade. He was very brave for a human. Brave enough to live close to my tree when many others had fled. Brave enough even to trade.

I strolled along below his wooden boundary fence, but the moment I reached the farmyard flags, I blew myself up to the size that works best with most humans. Not big enough to be too intimidating, but not small enough to give Old Rowler ideas. In fact, exactly the same size as the farmer had been before his old bones had started to weaken, his spine to bend.

I rapped on the door softly. It was my special rhythmical rap. Not loud enough to wake his three daughters but audible enough to bring the farmer huffing and puffing down the stairs.

He opened the door no more than the width of his calloused hand. Then he held a candle to the crack so that it lit up my face.

'What is it this time?' he demanded belligerently. 'I hoped I'd seen the last of you. It's months since you last bothered me. I was hoping you'd never wake up again!'

'I'm thirsty,' I said, 'and it's too early to hunt. I need a little something to warm my belly for a few hours.' Then I smiled, showing my sharp teeth and allowing my hot breath to steam upwards into the cold air.

'I've nothing to spare. Times are hard,' protested the farmer. 'It's been one of the hardest winters I can remember. I've lost cattle – even sheep.'

'How are your three daughters keeping? I hope they're well,' I asked, opening my mouth a little wider.

The candle began to dance and shake in Old Rowler's hands, just as I'd expected.

'You keep away from my daughters, Slither. D'ye hear? Keep away.'

'I was only enquiring after their health.' I softened my voice. 'How's the youngest one? I hope her cough's better now.'

'Don't waste my time!' he snapped. 'What are ye here for?'

'I need blood. Bleed a bullock for me – just a little blood to set me up. You can spare half a cup.'

'I told you, it's been a long hard winter,' he said. 'It's a bad time and the surviving animals need all their strength to get through.'

Seeing that I wouldn't get something for nothing, I drew a coin from the pocket of my coat and held it so that it gleamed in the candlelight.

Old Rowler watched as I spat onto the flank of the bullock to deaden the feeling there; so that when I made a small, precise cut in the hide, the animal wouldn't feel a thing. The blood soon began to flow, and I caught it in the metal cup that the farmer had provided, not wasting a single drop.

'I wouldn't really harm your daughters, you know,' I said. 'They've become almost like a family to me.'

'Your kind know nothing about families,' he muttered. 'You'd eat your own mother if you were hungry enough. What about Brian Jenson's daughter from the farm near the river? She disappeared early last spring, never to be seen again. Too many of my neighbours have suffered at your hands.'

I didn't bother to deny his accusation, but neither did I confirm it. Sometimes accidents happened. Mostly I control my taking, husbanding the resources of my haizda, but occasionally the urge gets the better of me and I take too much blood.

'Hey! Hang on a minute – we agreed on half a cup,' Old Rowler protested.

I smiled and pressed my fingers against the wound so that the blood immediately stopped flowing. 'So we did,' I agreed. 'Still, three quarters of a cup's not too bad. It's a good compromise.'

I took a long drink, my eyes never leaving the farmer's face. He wore a long overcoat and I knew that its lining concealed a wickedly sharp sabre. If sufficiently threatened or provoked, the old man wouldn't hesitate to use it. Not that Rowler, even with his sabre, posed any real threat to me, but it would bring our trade to a close. And that would be a pity because they were useful, men like him. I preferred to hunt, obviously, but the keeping of bloodstock – especially bullocks, which were my favourite – made things easier when times were hard. I wasn't prepared to keep them myself, but I did appreciate the place of this farmer in the scheme of things. He was the only one in my haizda that I ever traded with.

Perhaps I was getting old? Once I would have ripped out the throat of a human such as Rowler – ripped it out without a moment's thought. But I was past my first flush of youth and well-advanced in the magecraft of the haizda. Already I was an adept.

But this, my two hundredth summer, was a dangerous time for a haizda mage – the time when we sometimes fall victim to what we call *skaiium*. You see, living so long changes the way you think. You become more mellow, more understanding of the feelings and needs of others. That's bad for a haizda mage, and many of us don't survive these dangerous years because they lead to a softening of the blood-lust, a dulling of the teeth.

So I knew I had to be careful.

The warm blood flowed down my throat and into my stomach, filling me with new strength. I smiled and licked my lips.

I'd no need to hunt for at least another day, so I handed the cup back to Old Rowler and headed directly for my favourite spot. It was a clearing in the small wood, on the southern slopes that overlooked the farm. Then I shrank myself down, coat and boots included, to my smallest size, the one I often use for sleeping. Now I was no larger than a grey-whiskered sewer rat.

The ox blood, however, remained exactly the same size, so

that my stomach now felt very full. Despite the fact that I'd only just woken up, the combination of a very full stomach and the newly risen sun made me feel very sleepy indeed.

So I lay on my back and stretched out. My overcoat has a special slit, like a very short sleeve, to allow my tail out into the air. When I'm running, hunting or fighting, it coils up my back very tightly, but sometimes in summer, when the sun is shining and I'm feeling sleepy, I lie down on the warm grass and let it stretch out behind me. Happy and relaxed, I did that now, and in no time at all I was fast asleep.

Normally, with a stomach as full as that, I'd have slept soundly for a day and a night, but just before sunset, a scream cut through the air like a blade, waking me suddenly.

I sat up but then remained very still. My nostrils dilated and twitched as I began to sniff the air.

Blood . . .

I raised my tail and used it to gather more information. Things couldn't have been better and my mouth began to water. Ox blood was sweet and delicious, but this was the most appetizing blood of all. It was freshly spilled human blood and it came from the direction of Old Rowler's farm.

Instantly my thirst returned; I quickly got to my feet and began to run towards the distant fence. My long loping strides soon brought me to the boundary and, once under the fence, I immediately grew to human size. I used my tail again, searching for the source of the blood. It came from the North Pasture, and now I knew exactly whose it was.

I'd been close enough to the old man to smell it through his wrinkled skin, to hear it pounding along his knotted veins. Old blood it might be, but where human blood was concerned I couldn't be too choosy.

Yes, it was Old Rowler. He was bleeding.

Then I detected another source of blood, though this was far weaker. It was the scent of a young human female.

I began to run again, my heart pounding with excitement.

When I reached the North Pasture, the sun was an orange globe sitting precisely upon the tip of the horizon. One glance and I understood everything.

Old Rowler lay sprawled like a broken doll close to the trunk of a yew tree. Even from this distance I could see the blood on the grass. A figure was bending over him. It was a girl in a brown dress, a girl with long hair the colour of midnight. I sensed her young blood too. It was sweeter and more enticing than Old Rowler's.

It was Nessa, his eldest daughter. I could hear her sobs as she tended to the old man. Then I saw the bull in the next field. It was stamping its feet angrily and tossing its horns. It must have gored the farmer who, despite his injury, had managed to stagger through the gate and close it behind him.

Suddenly the girl looked back over her shoulder and saw me. With a little cry of terror she rose to her feet, pulled up her long skirt above her knees and began to run away towards the house. I could have caught her easily, but I had all the time in the world now, so I began to walk towards the crumpled body.

At first I thought that the old man was dead, but my sharp ears detected the faltering rhythm of a failing heart. Old Rowler was dying, for sure: there was a massive hole beneath his ribs and his blood was still bubbling out onto the grass.

As I knelt down beside him, he opened both eyes. His face was twisted with pain but he tried to speak. I had to bend closer, until my left ear was almost touching the old man's blood-flecked lips.

'My daughters . . .' he whispered.

'Don't you go worrying about your daughters,' I said.

'But I do worry,' said the dying farmer. 'Do ye remember the terms of the first trade we made?'

I didn't reply but I remembered them all right. The trade had taken place seven years earlier when Nessa had just turned ten.

'While I live, keep away from my three daughters!' he'd warned. 'But if anything ever happens to me, you can have the eldest, Nessa, in return for taking the other two south to their aunt and uncle in Pwodente. They live in the village of Stoneleigh, close to the last bridge before the Western Sea . . .'

'I'll take care of them,' I'd promised, realizing that this could be the beginning of years of useful trade with the farmer. 'Treat 'em like family.'

'A trade,' the old man had insisted. 'Is it a trade?'

'Yes,' I'd agreed. 'It's a trade.'

It had been a good trade because, according to the law of Bindos, each Kobalos citizen has to sell in the slave markets at least one purra – or human girl – every forty years or become an outcast, shunned by his fellows and slain on sight. As a haizda mage, I did not normally dabble in the markets and did not wish to own females in the customary way. But I knew that the time would come when I must meet my next obligation or suffer the consequences. Otherwise I would become an outlaw, hunted down by my own people. Rowler was old; once he was dead I could sell Nessa.

And now here he was before me, dying, and Nessa was mine.

The farmer began to cough up a dark clot of phlegm and blood. He hadn't long now. Within moments he'd be dead.

It would take a week at most to deliver the two younger girls to their relatives. Then Nessa would belong to me. I could force her north to the slave market, taking my time while I sampled some of her blood on the way.

Suddenly the old man began to fumble in the pocket of his overcoat. Perhaps he was searching for a weapon, I thought.

But he pulled out a little brown notebook and a pencil. With shaking hands, not even looking at the page, he began to scribble. He scribbled a lot of words for a dying man. When he'd finished, he tore out the page and held it towards me. Cautiously, I moved closer and accepted the note.

'It's to Nessa,' Rowler whispered. 'I've told her what she has to do. You can have everything – the farm, the animals and Nessa. Remember what we agreed? All you have to do is get Susan and Bryony to their aunt and uncle. Will you keep to our trade? Will ye do it?'

I read the note quickly. When I'd finished, I folded it in two and pushed it into my overcoat pocket. Then I smiled, showing just a hint of teeth. 'We made a trade and I'm honour-bound to keep to it,' I said.

Then I waited with Old Rowler until he died. It took longer

than I expected. He struggled for breath and seemed reluctant to go, even though he was in great pain. The sun had sunk well below the horizon before he gave a final shudder.

I watched him very carefully, my curiosity aroused. I had traded with Old Rowler for seven years, but flesh and blood is opaque and hides the true nature of the soul within. I had often wondered about this stubborn, brave but sometimes cantankerous old farmer. Now, at last, I would finally find out exactly what he was.

I was waiting to see his soul leave his body, and I wasn't disappointed.

A grey shape began to materialize above the crumpled over-coat. It was very faint and ever so slightly luminous. It was helical in form, a faint spiral, and much, much smaller than Old Rowler. I'd often watched human souls before and I liked to wait and see which way they would go.

So what was Old Rowler?

Was he an 'Up' or a 'Down'?

I harvest souls and draw power from them, absorbing them into my own spirit. So I prepared myself to reach out and snatch the farmer's soul. It was a difficult thing to do and, even with the whole force of my concentration, could only be accomplished if the soul lingered a while. But this soul did not tarry.

With a faint whistle it began to spiral away, spinning up into the sky. Not many did that. Usually they gave a sort of groan or howl and plunged into the earth. So Old Rowler was clearly an Up. I'd missed out on a new soul, but what did that matter? He was gone now and my curiosity was satisfied.

I began to search the body. There was only one coin. Probably the same one I'd given him earlier for the ox blood. Next I pulled out the sabre. The handle was a little rusty but I liked the balance and the blade was sharp.

I swished it through the air a few times. It had a good feel to it so I thrust it safely into the lining of my own overcoat.

That done, I was free to begin the main business of the night.

Old Rowler's daughters . . .

It was getting dark when I reached the farmhouse. There'd be no moon tonight and there was only one light coming from the house – the faint, fitful flicker of a candle behind the tattered curtains of the front bedroom.

I loped up to the door and rapped loudly upon it three times. I used the black knocker, the one decorated with the one-eyed head of a gargoyle, which was supposed to frighten off anything threatening that approached by night. Of course, this was just superstitious nonsense and my triple rap echoed through the house.

There was no reply. Those three girls had no manners, I thought. No manners at all.

Angrily, I dropped on all fours and ran three times round the house in a widdershins direction, against the clock, and each time I passed the front door I let out a loud, intimidating howl.

Next I returned to the front of the house and blew myself up to three times human size. I placed my forehead against the cold glass of the bedroom window and closed one eye.

With my left eye, I could just see through the narrow chink where the curtains met. I spotted Nessa, my inheritance, and her two sisters, huddled together on the bed.

Nessa was in the middle, with her arms wrapped about the shoulders of her younger sisters, Susan and Bryony. I'd spied on them many times before. There wasn't much I didn't know about these girls.

Nessa was seventeen, Susan a year younger. Susan was plumper than Nessa, with hair the colour of ripe corn. She would have fetched the best price at the slave market. As for Bryony, she was still a child, about eight summers old at the most; cooked very slowly, her flesh would be succulent, even tastier than day-old chicken – though many kobalos would prefer such young flesh raw.

The truth was that Nessa was worth the least of all, but her sale would allow me to fulfil my duties under the law of Bindos. A trade is a trade, and I always keep my word, so I shrank to human size and, with one almighty blow of my left hand, struck the front door.

The wood splintered, the house shook, the lock shattered and, with a groan, the old door swung back upon its hinges.

18

Then, without waiting for an invitation, I stepped across the threshold and climbed the wooden stairs.

❧NESSA❧

I felt ashamed at having left my father like that. I'd left him to die alone. But the terror of seeing the beast so close had over-whelmed me.

Having reached the safety of the house, I'd locked all the doors and then led Susan and Bryony up to my bedroom. My anguish and terror had rendered me almost speechless, but once there I could keep silent no longer.

'Father's dead!' I'd cried. 'He's dead – gored by the bull!'

My sisters both gave wails of grief. We'd climbed up onto the bed and I'd put my arms around them, trying to give what comfort I could. But then we heard the terrifying noises out-side the house. They began with three loud raps, quickly followed by a series of terrible blood-curdling howls which made the hairs on the back of my neck stand up.

'Cover your ears! Don't listen!' I urged my sisters. Of course, my arms were still around them so I was forced to endure the terrifying sounds. I thought I heard heavy breath-ing from outside the window, and for one awful moment it seemed as if a gigantic eye was peering through the gap in the curtain.

But how could that be? The beast was not that big. I'd glimpsed him on his visits to our farm and he'd seemed hardly taller than my poor father.

Next there came a terrible crash from below. I knew exactly

what it was and my heart began to beat even faster. The beast had smashed in the front door.

I heard heavy feet stamping up the stairs, approaching the bedroom door. It was locked, but the door was nowhere near as stout as the one the beast had already forced – it would prove no defence at all. My whole body began to shake.

The door handle slowly turned while I gaped at it in terror.

'Nessa,' the beast growled. 'Open the door and let me in. I'm your new father now. Be an obedient girl and let me in.'

I felt appalled at what he was saying. How could such a monster claim to be my father?

'Your old dead father left the farm to me, Nessa,' the beast continued. 'And he gave you to me. And if you're good to me, Nessa, then I'll be good to your two plump sisters. He asked me to take your sisters on a long journey to live in happiness with your aunt and uncle. I promised him I'd do that because I always keep my promises to the dead. But you belong to me, Nessa. So you have to be obedient. Why don't you answer? Don't you believe me? Well, read this, then. It's your father's will.'

I couldn't believe what he was saying. My sisters were whimpering in shock. How could my father have agreed to such a terrible thing? I wondered. I thought he'd loved me. Didn't he care about me at all?

The beast pushed a piece of paper under the door and I clambered off the bed, picked it up and started to read what was written.

To Nessa

I've promised the beast that he can have the farm and you. In return he's promised to deliver Bryony and Susan to your aunt and uncle. I've tried to be a good father and, had it ever proved necessary, I would have sacrificed myself for you. Now you must sacrifice yourself for your younger sisters.

Your loving father

Despite the shakiness of the letters, it was undoubtedly Father's handwriting, but I had to read it three times before its meaning sank into my befuddled brain. There were spots of blood on it – he must have written the letter in his final living moments.

I couldn't think straight, but I knew that I had to get the beast out of the house. If I didn't agree to what my father had written, the dreadful creature would smash down the bedroom door and perhaps kill all three of us. So I took a deep breath to calm myself before speaking.

'I accept the terms of my father's will,' I said. 'But my sisters are terrified. I want you to go away and leave us alone for a while. Please stay away from the farm.'

'I'll do that, Nessa,' the beast replied, surprising me with his agreement. 'No doubt you'll need some time to get over your father's death. But you must come and visit me tomorrow just before sunset. I live in the largest ghanbala tree on the far side of the river. You can't miss it. There we'll talk about what has to be done.'

*

The following day I set off to keep my promise. I was terrified, and having to visit the beast at dusk only made it worse. I'd spent the day doing my usual farm chores in addition to those tasks usually performed by my father. Despite that, I hadn't been able to keep at bay my fear of what was to come. Soon it would be dark and I would be alone with the monster and totally at his mercy.

Neighbours had gone missing from time to time – something my father would never comment on. Once I had asked him whether he thought the beast was responsible.

'Never speak of such things again, daughter!' he had warned. 'We are safe in our own house, so be grateful for that.'

But now we were no longer safe in that house. If I did not visit the lair of the beast, he would return to our farm. What could be more terrifying than that?

Perhaps he would devour me on the spot. After all, my father had given me into his ownership in return for the safety of my two sisters.

I had told Bryony and Susan that, if I failed to return by dawn, they should flee to the house of a neighbour on the other side of the valley. But even there they wouldn't be safe if the beast failed to keep his word.

I reached the river bank and approached the fording place. There was no doubt about the location of his lair. He was right: I couldn't miss it. It was twice as big as any other tree in the vicinity – a gigantic ghanbala with a trunk of a tremendous girth, its huge twisted branches stark against the fading light.

22

I approached the tree, and as I moved closer to that vast trunk, it grew darker, the branches gathering above me to block out the last of the light from the sky. Suddenly there was a soft thud behind me and I whirled round in terror to face the beast.

'Hello, Nessa,' he said, giving me a hideous smile that revealed his sharp teeth. 'What a good, dutiful daughter you are to keep your promise. Tomorrow, just to show you how grateful I am, I'll bury your poor father's body before the rats can spoil it too much. The eyes have gone already, I'm afraid, though he won't be needing them now. But sadly those aren't the only things he was missing: the rats had already nibbled off two of his toes and three of his fingers. Still, his body will soon be in the ground and I'll cover his grave with rocks so that it won't be dug up by a hungry animal, don't you worry. He'll be safe and snug in the dark, being slowly eaten by worms, as is only right and proper.'

That cruel, callous reference to my father brought a lump to my throat and I could hardly breathe. I bowed my head and was unable to meet the monster's eyes, ashamed that I'd not plucked up the courage to go out and bury my father myself. When I looked up, he gave another grotesque grin, pulled a key from his pocket, spat upon it three times, and inserted it into a lock in the trunk of the tree.

'This is a door I use only rarely,' he said, 'but it's the only way to get you into the tree in one piece. Enter before me. You are my guest!'

Fearful that he might strike me down from behind, I never-theless turned my back on him and walked through the open doorway into the tree.

'Most guests are usually dead when I drag them in here, but you are special to me, Nessa, and I've done my best to brighten up the place for you.'

His words horrified me, and my heart began to palpitate, but I looked about me in astonishment. It was incredible to find such well-furnished quarters within a tree. There were thirteen candles, each in an ornate candlestick, set upon a dining table so highly polished that I could see my own reflection in it.

'Would you like a glass of wine, Nessa?' the beast asked in his gruff voice. 'Things always look better viewed through the bottom of a glass.'

I tried to refuse his offer, but when I opened my mouth I could only manage a gasp of fear. His words made me shiver because that was one of my father's sayings. In fact I could see that it was my father's wine. I knew that he'd sold ten bottles to the beast the previous autumn: they were all lined up on the table behind the two glasses.

'Wine is the next best thing to blood!' he said, showing me his teeth again. He'd opened all the bottles already and they were now just loosely corked. 'I'm feeling very thirsty and I hope you won't expect more than your fair share. Four bottles should be enough for a human, don't you agree?'

I shook my head, refusing the wine. But suddenly a little hope flared within me. If he was offering me wine, maybe he wasn't going to kill me now after all?

'It's good wine,' the beast commented. 'Your old father made it with his own hands. So I'll be only too happy to drink your share too. We wouldn't want to waste it, would we, little Nessa?'

Again I didn't speak, but began looking at the room in more detail, my eyes taking in everything: the bottles and jars on the rows and rows of shelves; the long table in the far corner of the room, decorated with what appeared to be the skulls of small animals and birds. My eyes stopped their wandering at the three lambskin rugs that adorned the floor. Each one was a most vivid shade of red. Surely that wasn't just dye . . . could it be blood?

'I see that you're admiring my rugs, little Nessa. It takes a lot of skill to keep them looking that way. Blood never wants to stay red for long outside a body.'

At those words I began to tremble from head to foot.

'The truth is, Nessa, I'd like to taste a little of your blood now.' I cringed away from the beast in fear, but he continued, 'However, you've shown good faith by coming to see me, making me believe that you will keep to the terms of the trade I made with your father. That's why I asked you here. And you have passed the test, satisfying me that you are a person of honour who can keep to an agreement. You have also been gracious enough to refuse the wine, so that now I have all ten bottles to myself. So I am going to let you go home.

'Be ready at sunset tomorrow,' he told me as I started to breathe a little more easily. 'Kill and salt three pigs, but collect every last drop of blood and fill a milk churn with it – the journey will make me very thirsty. Pack up cheese and bread and candles and two large cooking pots. Oil the wheels of your largest cart. I'll bring horses, but you must provide the oats. And take plenty of warm clothes and blankets. There might be snow before the week is out. We will take your two sisters to their relatives, as I promised. Once that is done, I will take you north and sell you in the slave market. Your life will be short but useful to my people.'

I walked slowly home, numbed by what I had learned. But there were practicalities to consider, such as dealing with the farm animals. They would be best given to one of our neighbours. I had a lot to arrange before my life changed utterly. I was going to become a slave of the beasts and would surely not survive for very long.

CHAPTER
3
THE DARK TOWER

I arrived at the farm at sunset, as promised, and was pleased to find the three Rowler sisters ready for the journey.

Three stout trunks waited in the yard, and upon the smallest sat Bryony, nervously picking the loose threads from her woollen gloves. Susan was standing behind Bryony, her mouth pulled down into a pouty sulk, while Nessa paced up and down impatiently. It was getting colder by the minute. They had sensibly chosen to wear their warmest woollen dresses, but their coats were thin and threadbare, offering little protection against the cold.

I halted at the open gate and stared at the girls, almost drooling. And on looking more closely, I saw that the flesh of the youngest sister would be very tender and best eaten uncooked; even raw it would melt off the bone. As for Susan, there was plenty of meat on her older bones, but I knew that her blood would be even better. I would need all the discipline I could muster to keep to the terms of my deal with the dead farmer.

Dismissing such thoughts from my head, I urged my black stallion into the yard, his hooves clattering on the flags. Behind me I led a white mare and a heavy shire horse for drawing a cart in which the two younger sisters could ride. I had stolen all three horses that very day.

I circled the yard three times before coming to a halt, then leaned down and showed my teeth in a wide smile. Terror flickered upon the faces of Bryony and Susan, but Nessa walked boldly up to me and pointed towards the shed just beyond the stables.

'The cart's in there,' she said, her chin raised defiantly. 'It's already loaded with the provisions, but the trunks were too heavy for us . . .'

I leaped down from my horse and flexed my hairy fingers close to Nessa's face, making the bones crack. Then, in no time at all, I harnessed the shire horse to the cart before tossing up the three trunks – feeble humans; the trunks were as light as air.

Then I smirked when Nessa noticed the freshly sharpened sabre at my belt, the one that had belonged to her father.

'That is my father's sword!' she protested, her eyes widening.

'He won't be needing it now, little Nessa,' I told her.

'Anyway, we have no time to waste dwelling on the past. This white mare's for you. Chose it specially, I did.'

'Are my sisters to ride in the cart?' she asked.

'Of course – they will find it far better than walking!' I declared.

'But Susan has no experience in handling a horse and cart, and the going may become difficult,' Nessa protested.

'Fear not, little Nessa: the shire horse will be obedient to my will and your sisters will come to no harm. They can simply sit in the back of the cart.'

It had been but the work of a minute to breathe into the nostrils of the big horse and use my magic to claim its obedience. It would follow in my wake, moving only when I moved and halting when I brought my own mount to a stop.

'You said you would bury my father,' Nessa accused suddenly, 'but his body was still lying there. Don't you worry – I did it myself with the help of my sisters. However, it suggests to me that you don't keep your promises, after all.'

'I always keep to a trade, Nessa – but that was no such thing, merely a kind offer that I meant to carry out. Unfortunately I've been busy getting hold of these horses and didn't have time. It was better that you should bury him though. It might make up for running away and leaving him to die alone.'

Nessa didn't answer but a tear ran down each cheek and she quickly turned her back on me and struggled up into the saddle while her sisters climbed into the cart. As we rode down the track towards the crossroads, the air grew even colder and frost began to whiten the grass.

It had been difficult obtaining three horses at such short notice. I avoid killing or stealing within my own haizda, so had been forced to range far beyond it to acquire the mounts.

I hoped that Nessa wouldn't notice the dark bloodstain on the left flank of the white mare.

There had been conflict between my people and humans for at least five thousand years. At times, during periods of Kobalos expansion, it had flared up into outright war. Now it was merely a simmering hostility.

My private domain, my haizda, is large, containing many farms and a number of small settlements which I husband and control. But once beyond its borders I become a lone enemy, likely to attract all sorts of unwelcome attention. No doubt, seeing the purrai in my possession, humans would band together and attempt to take them from me by force. For that reason it was necessary to be vigilant and travel mostly by night.

Just before dawn on the third day, it began to snow.

At first the dusting was very light, hardly adding to the white coating of frost. But the snow persisted, grew heavier, and the wind started to blow hard from the west.

'We can't travel in these conditions,' Nessa protested. 'We'll get trapped in a drift and freeze to death!'

'There is no choice,' I insisted. 'We must go on. I am hardy and can endure, but if we stop now, you poor weak humans will die!'

Despite my words I knew that the weather would soon bring us to a halt. The girls couldn't survive more than a few days in these conditions so I was forced to change my plans.

Although the heavens were now lit with the grey light of dawn, I decided to take a risk, and after a short rest we continued on our way. We headed west now, rather than south, right into the teeth of what had become a blizzard.

At first Susan and Bryony sat cowering under the tarpaulin in the back of the open cart; both kept complaining of the cold, but I could hardly blame them for that. Then, after an hour or so, they said that when sheltering from the weather under the tarpaulin, the movement of the cart made them feel sick, so for the rest of the day they kept their heads above it, exposed to the bitter cold and damp of the blizzard. It was only a matter of time before they froze to death.

As the light began to fail, we were moving through a dense wood of spruce and pine, heading down a slope towards a frozen stream with an even steeper slope rising beyond it.

'We'll never get our horses up that incline!' Nessa shouted. She was right.

At the bottom on the left stood a five-barred gate. Here, giving the purra a wicked grin, I dismounted. After a good deal of scooping of snow and pulling and tugging, I managed to open it wide enough for the horse and cart to pass through.

A cinder track ran alongside the stream, and upon this the snow had been unable to take a hold: each snowflake had melted immediately on making contact. The track was actually steaming.

I watched Nessa dismount and lead her own mare through the gate. She reached down to test the surface with her fingers.

'It's hot!' she squealed, drawing her fingers away rapidly.

'Of course it is!' I said with a laugh. 'How else could it be kept free of snow?'

Nessa walked back to the cart and spoke to her sisters. 'Are you all right?' she asked.

'I'm so cold,' Susan complained, 'I can hardly feel my hands or the nose on my face.'

'I feel sick, Nessa. Can we stop soon?' Bryony asked.

Nessa didn't reply but looked up at me. 'Where are we going?'

'A hostelry,' I replied and, without bothering to elaborate, I leaped back onto my horse and took up the lead once again.

The spruce and pine gave way to deciduous sycamore, oak and ash trees, which were waiting, bereft of leaves, for the coming of the short summer. These trees pressed in upon us, dark and thick, their stark branches hooked like talons against the grey sky. It was strange to see such trees so far north.

Soon there came a strange silence: the wind suddenly died away, and even the clop of hooves and the rattle of the cart-wheels seemed muffled on the cinders.

Bryony, the youngest child, started to sob with cold. Before Nessa could ride closer to offer her words of comfort, I turned and hissed at her to ensure her silence, placing my finger vertically against my lips.

After another few moments, I saw through the trees a faint purple light that blinked on and off like the opening and closing of a giant eye. Finally a building came into view.

It was a dark tower, enclosed by a high circular wall complete with battlements, and a portcullis that could only be reached by means of a drawbridge crossing a wide moat.

'Is this what you call a hostelry?' Nessa demanded angrily. 'I'd hoped for an inn with welcoming fires and clean rooms where we might take refuge from the blizzard and sleep in comfort. My sisters are half frozen to death. What is this strange forbidding tower? It seems to have been constructed by other than human hands.'

The tower itself was about nine storeys high and the size of three or more large farmhouses combined. It was built of a dark purple stone, and the whole structure gleamed as rivulets of water cascaded down its sides. For, although snow was still falling heavily from the darkening sky, all around the tower the ground was completely clear. Both walls and ground were steaming, as if some huge fire burned deep within the earth. The fortress had been constructed over a hot-spot, an underground geyser that heated the stones of the tower.

I had spent a night in this tower almost forty years earlier, on my way to sell a slave and meet my legal obligations under the law of Bindos. However, at that time it had been ruled by someone who was now dead, slain by Nunc, the High Mage who was the tower's present incumbent.

I smiled at Nessa. 'It is not a hostelry for your kind. But beggars can't be choosers. This is a *kulad*, a fortress built by my people. Better stay close to me if you wish to survive the night.'

As we moved forward, I heard gasps from the two younger sisters, and the portcullis began to rise. The sound of chain and ratchet could clearly be heard, but there was no gatekeeper, and nobody came out to either greet or challenge us.

I guided the purrai across the circular inner courtyard towards stables with fresh straw for the horses and a lean-to under which the cart could be sheltered from the worst of the elements. Then I led them through a narrow door to a spiral staircase that rose widdershins up and up, into the dark inner tower. Every ten steps there were torches set within iron holders bolted to the wall. Their yellow flames danced and flickered, although the air was perfectly still, but they were never enough to dispel the shadows that gathered above them.

'I don't like this place,' Bryony whimpered. 'I can feel eyes watching us. Horrible things hiding in the darkness!'

'There's nothing here to worry about,' Nessa told her. 'It's just your imagination.'

'But there could be insects and mice,' Susan complained. Succulent she might be, but that purra's voice was starting to irritate me.

We began to climb the stairs; wooden doors were spaced at intervals, but then we came to three set quite close together, so I chose these for the sisters. Each had a rusty iron lock into which was inserted a large steel key.

'Here's a warm bedroom for each of you,' I said, my tail rising in annoyance. 'You'll be safe enough in here if I lock the doors. Try to sleep. There's no supper, but breakfast will be served soon after dawn.'

'Why can't we all just share a room?' demanded Nessa.

'Too small,' I said, opening the first of the doors. 'And each has only one bed. Young growing girls like you need your rest.'

Nessa looked in and I saw the dismay on her face. It was indeed small and cramped.

'It's dirty in there,' Susan complained with a pout.

Bryony began to cry softly. 'I want to stay with Nessa! I want to stay with Nessa!'

'Please allow Bryony to share my room,' said Nessa, making one last desperate appeal. 'She's too young to be left alone in a place like this . . .'

But I paid no heed and, twisting my face into a savage expression, pushed her roughly inside. Next I slammed the door behind her and twisted the key to lock her in. I quickly did the same for each of her sisters.

But although cruelty is in my nature, it was not this that prompted my behaviour now. I had done it for their own safety, confining each separately to mark them as three distinct items of my property, according to the customs of my people.

I'd had no choice but to bring the three girls here – they would soon have died of exposure outside. We were now well beyond the last human habitation and this was the only refuge that was available. It was a dangerous place, even for a haizda mage, and I could not be sure of a welcome. Now, as was customary, I had to ascend to the top of the tower to make obeisance to its lord, Nunc. He had a formidable reputation and ruled by fear.

He was a High Mage, the most powerful rank of Kobalos mage. As outsiders who dwell within our own individual territories far from Valkarky, we haizdas do not fit within that hierarchy of mages. I do not fear a High Mage, but would if necessary make obeisance to him. If I were forced to fight him, I was not sure what the outcome would be. Nevertheless I was curious to meet Nunc in the flesh and see if he lived up to the stories told about him. It was said that, in a raid against a human kingdom, he had devoured the monarch's seven sons in front of him before tearing off that unfortunate king's head with his bare hands.

As I climbed the spiral staircase, the air grew warmer and more humid and my discomfort grew. Such was the peculiarity of the High Mages that they sometimes actively sought out a harsh environment in order to prove their hardiness.

Even though I was now within sight of the top landing, no guards were visible. Yet my tail told me that many of Nunc's servants were nearby, in the subterranean areas beneath the tower.

There was only one door on the landing, and I pushed it open. I found myself in the anteroom. This was a bath house where Nunc's servants and guests could cleanse their bodies before proceeding further. However, I'd never seen one quite like this. In such rooms, the water was often uncomfortably warm, but the temperature here was extreme. The air was full of suffocating steam and I immediately began to struggle for breath.

The entire room, but for a perimeter strip of stone and a narrow arch that provided a bridge to the far side, was given over to a huge sunken bath filled with water so hot that it was generating steam as I watched.

Nunc, the High Mage, was immersed in the bath up to his armpits, but his knees were visible, and upon each he rested a huge hairy hand. His face was very full, and shaved according to the custom of Kobalos mages. The short stubble was black, but for a long grey patch low on his forehead – a duelling scar of which he was very proud.

Although Nunc was huge – half as big again as me – I felt not in the least threatened by his bulk. Size was relative, and as a haizda I could, in a moment, blow myself up to an equal size.

'Enter the water, guest,' Nunc boomed. 'My house is your house. My purrai are your purrai.'

Nunc had addressed me in Baelic, the ordinary informal tongue of the Kobalos people; it was years since I'd last heard it and the language sounded strange, almost as if the time I'd spent near humans had made my own people now seem alien. Immediately it made me wary. I had never met Nunc before, and for a Kobalos to speak to a stranger in Baelic implied warmth and friendship, but worryingly was frequently used before offering to trade. I had nothing I could barter.

I bowed and, after removing my belt and sabre, which I carefully positioned against the wall, undid the thirteen buttons of my coat and hung it on one of the hooks on the back of the door. It was somewhat heavier than usual, for the lining contained the three keys to the girls' rooms. Next, I removed the diagonal straps and scabbards with the two short blades and set them down next to the sabre.

Finally I tugged off my boots and prepared to enter the water. It would take great concentration and willpower for me to endure such a boiling temperature, but I had to immerse myself, if only for a short time, in order to comply with the customs of hospitality. I must not give Nunc an excuse to act against me in any way.

The water was very uncomfortable, but I slid in, forcing myself to put up with it. However, other thoughts were already disturbing my concentration. I remembered Nunc's greeting and was suddenly dismayed by his reference to purrai.

Purrai are human females, usually bred within the skleech pens of Valkarky – sometimes for slavery but mostly to be eaten. The term can also apply to human females such as the three sisters. That Nunc should keep purrai in this tower was of little surprise, but to offer them so promptly to a guest showed disrespect. This, in conjunction with his use of Baelic, suggested that he did indeed wish to trade.

Nunc's next words immediately confirmed that I was right.

'I offer you my three most prized purrai, but I require something of you in exchange – a trade. You must give your own purrai into my possession.'

'With the utmost courtesy and respect, I must decline your generous offer,' I told him. 'I am bound by a promise I made. I must deliver my three purrai to their relatives in Pwodente.'

Nunc growled deep in his throat. 'Any promise made to a human has no validity here – as High Mage I require your obedience in this matter. I need the youngest child this night at the feast of Talkus the Unborn. Such young tasty flesh will grace the occasion.'

'Although I respect your position, Lord,' I said, keeping my voice polite and deferential, 'I owe you no personal allegiance. The purrai are my property and I have the natural right under Kobalos law to dispose of them as I think fit. So I am sorry, but must reject your offer to trade.'

It was true that I had to respect Nunc as a High Mage, but I was perfectly entitled to refuse his demand. There the matter should have ended, but no sooner had I spoken than I felt a sudden sharp pain in my left leg, close to the ankle. It was as if someone had pricked my flesh with the point of a blade and twisted.

Instinctively, I reached down and touched something that eluded my grasp and undulated quickly away through the water.

I cursed my own stupidity, realizing that I'd been bitten by some kind of water snake. The heat and the steam had dulled my senses; otherwise I would have become aware of the creature upon entering the anteroom. Had I raised my tail, I would have detected it for sure, but such an act was unthinkable; it would have been a serious breach of etiquette and a great insult to my host. I had never expected such treachery.

Fearing for my life, I turned and tried to clamber out of the pool.

But it was already too late. I slipped back into the water, aware that my body was rapidly becoming numb. It was already difficult to breathe and my chest was growing even tighter.

'You are dying,' said Nunc, his deep voice booming back from the walls. 'You should have accepted my offer. Now your purrai are mine and I need give you nothing in return.'

Shuddering with pain, I fell into an intense darkness. I was not afraid to die, but I felt deep shame at having been bested so easily. I had made a mistake in underestimating Nunc. Skaiium had crept up on me almost without my noticing. I truly had grown soft. I was no longer fit to be a haizda mage.

CHAPTER
4
THE KOBALOS BEAST

≈NESSA≈

*Y*ou must be brave, Nessa, I told myself. *If ever you needed courage,
you need it now – for your own sake but most of all for your sisters'!*

I had been locked in a small oblong room without a
window. There was the stub of a candle impaled upon a rusty
spike protruding from the wall, and by its flickering light I
examined my surroundings.

My heart sank in dismay for, in truth, this was nothing more
than a cell; there was no furniture – just a heap of dirty straw
in the far corner.

I could see dark stains on the stone walls, as if some liquid
had been splashed there, and I feared it might be blood. I

shivered and looked more closely, and immediately felt heat radiating from the wall. At least I wouldn't be cold. That was a small comfort.

A hole in the floor with a rusty metal lid served to meet the needs of bodily functions; and there was a pitcher of water but no food.

For a moment, as I took stock of my surroundings, I felt despair, but that was quickly replaced by anger.

Why should my life be over before it had properly begun?

The deep sorrow that I had experienced at the sudden death of my father had transformed itself into a permanent ache of loss. I loved him, but I was so angry. Had he not thought of my feelings? What had he said in his letter?

Had it ever proved necessary, I would have sacrificed myself for you. Now you must sacrifice yourself for your younger sisters.

How presumptuous of him to command me to sacrifice myself for my sisters! How easy it was for him to say that! That sacrifice had never been demanded of him. He was now dead and free of this awful world. My pain was only just starting. I would become a slave of these beasts. I would never have a family of my own – no husband and children for me.

I checked the door, but there was no handle on the inside and I'd heard the key turn in the lock. There was no way out of the cell. I began to cry softly, but it was not self-pity that replaced my anger; I wept for my sisters – poor Bryony would be terrified, confined in a cell like this alone.

How quickly we'd fallen from relative happiness to this state of misery. Our mother had died giving birth to Bryony, but since that sad day Father had done his very best, providing for us and bravely trading with the Kobalos beast – Slither, he called it – to keep it at bay. We'd had little contact with the nearby village and other farms, but enough to know of the beast's reign of terror and to realize that we had been spared the fear and suffering that others in the neighbourhood had endured.

I thought I could hear Bryony crying out in the next cell, but when I placed my ear to the wall there was only silence.

I called out her name as loudly as I could – and then a second time. After each attempt I listened carefully with my ear against the wall. But there was no reply that I could hear.

After a while my candle guttered out, plunging me into darkness, and again I thought of Bryony. No doubt her candle would do the same and she'd be terrified. She had always been afraid of the dark.

Eventually I fell asleep, but was suddenly awoken by the sound of a key turning in the lock. The door groaned on its hinges and slowly opened, filling the cell with yellow light.

I fully expected to see Slither, and I tensed, preparing myself for whatever happened next. However, it was a young woman, who was standing in the open doorway brandishing a torch and beckoning me with her other arm.

She was the first human, apart from my sisters, that I had seen since leaving the farm. 'Oh, thank you!' I cried. 'My sisters—' But my smile of relief froze on my face when I saw the fierce expression in her eyes. She was not here as a friend.

Her bare arms were covered in scars. Some were a livid red and quite recent. Four other women stood behind her; two of them had multiple scars on their cheeks. Why should that be? Did they fight amongst themselves? I wondered. Three were carrying cudgels; the fourth brandished a whip. They were all quite young, but their eyes were full of anger, and their faces were very pale, as if they'd never seen sunlight.

I rose to my feet. The woman beckoned again and, when I hesitated, entered the cell, seized my forearm and dragged me roughly towards the door. I screamed out and tried to resist, but she was too strong.

Where were they taking me? I couldn't allow myself to be separated from my sisters. 'Susan! Bryony!' I yelled.

Outside, both arms were twisted up behind my back and I was forced up the steep flight of stone steps until, right at the very top, we came to a doorway. The women thrust me through it violently, making me lose my balance and sprawl onto the floor, which was smooth and warm to the touch. It was clad with ornate tiles, each depicting some exotic creature that could only have come from the artist's imagination. It was hot and humid within, the air full of steam, but ahead, as I got up onto my knees, I saw a huge bath sunk into the floor.

Once they'd pushed me inside, the women retreated back down the steps, first locking the door behind them. I climbed to my feet and stood with trembling legs, wondering what was going to happen next. Why had I been brought here?

Peering through the steam, I saw a narrow bridge leading over the bath to the foot of a great rusty iron door on the other side. Then I heard someone cry out in pain. That door filled me with foreboding. What lay beyond it?

My trembling became more violent and my heart sank, for it had sounded like Susan. Surely it couldn't be her? I hadn't heard a thing from my room. But when the cry came again, I was certain. What was happening to her? Someone was hurting her. The women must have dragged her up here too.

But why, when the beast had promised to protect us? Father had always claimed that he was a creature of his word – that he believed in what he called 'trade' and always honoured what he had promised. If that was so, how could he allow this to happen? Or could it be that he had lied – that *he* was the one inflicting the pain?

I walked along the edge of the bath. Then I halted and, for the first time, noticed the black coat on the hook behind the door and, beneath it, resting against the wall, the belt and the sabre that had once belonged to my father. Was Slither now on the other side of that door, hurting Susan?

I had to do something. My eyes skittered hither and thither, along the length of the room, looking anywhere but at the door. All at once I saw something dark in the bath close to the wall on my left. What was it? It looked like some dark furry animal floating face-down in the water.

The creature looked far too small to be the beast who called himself Slither – it was hardly a quarter of his bulk – but I remembered that my father had once told me how, by using dark magic, a haizda mage could change his size. Peeping through the curtains when he visited our farm, I had also seen some evidence of this, for the beast had indeed seemed to vary in size from day to day. I also remembered the huge eye that I had glimpsed through the chink in the curtain when Slither had visited the house after my father's death. I had assumed that it was the work of my own imagination, inspired by terror. But what if it really had been the beast? Could he really make himself that big? If so, he could surely also shrink.

But if this body was Slither's, then who had done this to him? How had he come to drown in this bath? Suddenly I thought I saw the beast's left foot twitch very slightly, and stepped closer.

Was he still alive? If he was, one part of me wanted to push him under the water and drown him. Nothing could please me more, and he was helpless now. I would never get a better chance than this to finish him off. But it wasn't possible. We were in a dangerous place, inhabited by more of these beasts. Without his protection, all three of us would die here.

So, without further thought, I knelt close to the water and, leaning across, grasped him firmly by the scruff of the neck.

Even as I did so, I saw something moving very rapidly through the water towards my hand; instinctively I released my burden and withdrew. It was a small black snake with three vivid yellow spots on top of its head. I had seen snakes in the fields but never one as striking as this.

I watched it undulate away, moving more slowly now, but it was hard to see through the steam. Knowing that it might circle back at any moment, I wasted no time, and now gripped the beast with both hands – at the base of the neck and low on his back – entwining my fingers in his fur. 'Come on!' I said to myself. And I tensed and pulled upwards with all my strength.

The bath was full almost to the brim, but even so I found it difficult to haul the creature out of the water. I made one final effort, and managed to drag him up onto the side of the bath, where I knelt, trembling with exertion. Again the scream came from beyond the door, and this time I was quite sure that it was the cry of Susan in torment.

'Please! Please!' she cried out. 'Don't do that! It hurts so much. Help me! Please help me or I'll die!'

My throat constricted in anguish. I couldn't bear the thought of one of these creatures hurting her.

Slither had promised to protect us: he was bound by that promise – without him we were completely at the mercy of the other inhabitants of the tower. But when I looked down at the bedraggled body, it displayed no sign of life at all, and I was filled with utter despair. Again there came a cry of pain and terror from Susan. In response, filled with anger at the hopelessness of everything and the pain of my sister, I began to beat Slither's body with my fists. As I did so, water oozed out of his mouth and formed a small brown puddle beside his head.

The colour of the liquid gave me an idea. I suddenly realized that there was, after all, one more thing that I could do, one final way in which he might possibly be revived.

Blood! Human blood! My father had once said that was the main source of Slither's power.

Quickly, I got to my feet and went over to the door where the beast's long black coat hung. There, I stooped and picked up the sabre that had once belonged to my father and carried it back to where the creature lay. Kneeling down, I turned him over.

My eyes swept upwards from his toes, noting with distaste the tangled forest of black fur. His mouth was open and his tongue lolled sideways over his teeth, hanging down almost as far as his left ear. The sight of him disgusted and repelled me.

Nervously, anticipating the pain, I positioned my arm just above Slither's mouth and, taking the sabre, made a quick cut into my flesh. The blade had been sharpened and sliced into my inner arm more deeply than I had intended. There was a sharp pain and a stinging sensation. And then my blood was falling like dark rain into the open mouth of the beast.

CHAPTER 5
I MUST FEED !

It was my fifth sense, that of taste, which drew me up out of that dark pit into which I had fallen. My mouth was full of warm, sweet blood.

I choked and spluttered, but then managed to swallow, and the rich liquid slid down into my belly, restoring me to life. My olfactory sense returned next. The inviting odour of the blood of a human female filled my nostrils. She was very close and was full of the same delicious blood that, even now, was filling my mouth.

The next sense to return was touch. It began with pins and needles in my extremities, which quickly became a fire, so that it felt as if my whole body were burning. It was then that my aural senses suddenly functioned once more and, hearing someone weeping, I opened my eyes and stared up in amazement at the figure of Nessa, who was crouching over me, tears running down her face. I saw the sabre gripped in her right hand. My mind was sluggish, and for a moment I thought she meant to strike me with it.

I tried to bring up my arms to defend myself, but I was too weak and couldn't even manage to roll away. But to my surprise she did not cut me. I lay there staring up at her, trying to make sense of what was happening.

Slowly I began to understand why she was holding the sword, finally linking its sharp edge to the blood falling towards me from the deep cut on her inner arm.

Then, as my memory returned, I recalled Nunc's treachery ... the bite of the water snake. I had died. Or so it had seemed. The blood was still falling into my mouth but there was less of it now. I swallowed again, then reached up, trying to seize Nessa's arm so that I could draw it down to my mouth. I needed more blood, but moved too slowly, and with a look of disgust, she snatched her arm out of reach.

By now the blood had done its job and I managed to roll over and rise up onto my knees, shaking myself violently like a dog so that water droplets scattered in all directions. My mind was working faster now. I was beginning to think. Beginning to realize the enormity of what Nessa had done for me.

She had given me her blood. And that human blood had strengthened my *shakamure* magic, counteracted the effects of the snake bite and drawn me back from the edge of death. But why had she done it? And why was she here and not still locked in the cell?

'My sister. Someone's hurting my sister through there. Help her, please!' Nessa begged, pointing to the door on the other side of the bridge. 'You promised we'd be safe . . .'

I heard another sound then. It was the distant whimper of a girl and it came from behind the door to Nunc's private quarters.

'She's been taken in there!' Nessa continued, her voice growing more frantic. 'And where's Bryony? Some awful women threw me in here and locked the door. I have just saved your life, so you owe me now! Help us, please!'

I stood shakily and raised my tail. With it I sensed Nunc and knew why Susan had cried out. He was drinking her blood. I was outraged that Nunc should flout Kobalos customs and avail himself of my property like this. But I was also filled with a sense of debt to Nessa. She was right: I owed her my life.

It was strange to acknowledge such a thing. A human female was nothing. Within the city of Valkarky she was just property. So why should I feel this way? What if it truly were skaiium, the softening of my predatory nature? Such a thing would indeed be terrible to bear.

I turned to face Nessa. I would kill Nunc and harden my nature again in the process. Nothing was more important.

'Give me the blade!' I commanded, simultaneously blowing myself up in size so that I was a head taller than the girl.

Weeping now, Nessa held it out towards me. Her hand was

shaking, but I saw that the blood had almost ceased flowing from her left arm and was beginning to coagulate. Rather than taking the blade then and there, I turned my back on the girl and went to get my coat and boots.

I pulled the boots on first, lacing them up carefully, then fastened the straps across my shoulders and chest, checking that the short blades were correctly positioned in the two scabbards. Next I drew on my coat, realizing as I did so that the three keys had been removed. As I fastened all thirteen buttons, Susan cried out again from beyond the door.

'Please – please hurry!' begged Nessa.

But I knew that it was important to avoid undue haste. Despite my anger I must move with caution, choosing my moment and striking only when the occasion permitted. Nunc was alone with the girl, but there might be up to three score warriors quartered below the tower, ready to defend their High Mage.

'So, who brought you here?' I asked, buckling on my belt. 'Not Kobalos warriors?'

'No. They were women.'

'How many?'

'There were five of them.'

I held my hand out for the sabre. So the purrai had brought Susan to Nunc so that he could drink her blood very slowly, savouring every sip. No doubt he had a different type of pleasure in mind when he dealt with Nessa because she was too skinny and her blood would be thin. He would have used her for blade practice, attempting to cut her as many times as possible without killing her. Eventually she would have died of shock and blood loss. By now, I was certain that the child, Bryony, would have already been given to the warriors to prepare for the feast.

I felt better now. I was stronger, but not yet strong enough. More blood would help. I knew that the most sensible course of action would be to take it from Nessa by force, but something within me resisted that alternative. Then I remembered the snake!

I went over to the edge of the bath and knelt down, immersing my hand in the steaming water.

'Be careful!' Nessa exclaimed. 'There's a snake in there!'

'That I know to my cost, little Nessa. It was responsible for putting me in the position you luckily found me in. Now it is the snake's turn to suffer!'

I'd probably been bitten by the small black snake known as a skulka, greatly feared because its bite induces a swift paralysis. It has the advantage for an assassin in that the presence of its venom in the blood is almost impossible to detect afterwards. Its victims become helpless the moment the poison has entered their bloodstream. Then they die in agony. No doubt Nunc had developed his immunity by gradual exposure to the toxin – the creature was probably his familiar.

My tail was standing erect on my back and, more accurately than eye or ear, it told me precisely where the snake was. It was undulating swiftly towards my hand now.

But just as the skulka opened its mouth, fangs ready to strike, I moved quickly and snatched it out of the water. I held it aloft,

gripping it below the head so that it could not bite me. Then –
to horrified gasps from Nessa – I bit off its head and spat it out
into the water, before sucking the blood from the body.

There wasn't anywhere near enough, so I tore off another
piece of snake and began to chew it carefully. The foolish girl
struggled to control her disgust. Couldn't she see that I did
what was necessary in order to save her sister? As I swallowed
the flesh, Susan cried out from beyond the door once again.

I turned and smiled at Nessa. 'Be patient, little Nessa. I need
strength. If I am weak, all of us will die.'

Only when I'd finished eating the whole snake did I cross the
narrow bridge and approach the rusty iron door. As I expected,
it was unlocked, so I pulled it open and stepped into a narrow
passageway which ended in a single door. This I also opened
and, with Nessa close on my heels, stepped boldly into Nunc's
private quarters.

This spacious room functioned as the study, private armoury
and bedroom of a Kobalos High Mage and, as such, was a
curious mixture of the spartan and the luxurious. Upon the
bare flags stood a large ornate oaken desk, its edges
embellished with the finest silver of a type I recognized
immediately. It was Combe-quality silver seized fifty-three
years earlier in a daring guerrilla raid deep into that human
territory far to the south. Nunc's exploits were well known. He
had achieved much but was known to be egotistical and had
worked to ensure that his fame spread.

On the far wall hung shields, axes, spears and blades of many
types, some very exotic, and beneath them stood a large table

covered with maps and piles of papers, held in place by large blue agate paperweights.

The rooms in my ghanbala tree also contain artefacts that are pleasing to look upon, but rather than this ostentatious display of maps and weapons, they represent my own interests: jars of herbs, ointments and preserved fauna and flora which add to my knowledge of the natural world and are useful to my magic.

Here the walls were panelled so extensively that not a trace of stone was visible; some were carved with representations of warriors in full combat armour, including the last King of Valkarky, who had been slain by an assassin.

I spotted Nunc, with Susan in his grasp, his teeth embedded in her neck. By now the girl was unconscious and it was Nessa who suddenly screamed behind me, alerting the High Mage to the threat I posed.

He released the child immediately and leaped backwards. As Susan crumpled to the floor, he seized a huge spear from the wall and brandished it aloft, directing it towards me. He had dressed formally in preparation for the feast, and was unfortunately wearing expensive chain-link armour that I judged thick enough to deflect a blade. But he had intended to eat, not fight, and thus his head and throat were bare and vulnerable to sharp steel.

'Lord Nunc!' I cried, my voice filled with anger. 'You have something of mine and now you must return it!'

As I spoke, I lifted my tail so that it stood up at my back and would give me early warning of my enemy's intentions. It was fortunate that I did so. There had been no visible indication that Nunc would attack – not even a twitch or the tensing of muscles – but by way of answer he hurled his spear directly at my head. As I have said, my tail had already alerted me to this and I was prepared. As the weapon sped towards me, I moved just one part of my body: I raised my arm and, using the broad flat of the sabre's blade, skilfully deflected the spear so that it struck the wall close to the door and crashed harmlessly to the stone flags.

Susan opened her eyes then and managed to kneel up on the floor, her eyes staring wildly at the scene about her. The moment she began to scream, Nunc ran over to the far wall, seized a sabre and a shield, and turned to face me.

He was evidently strong: the muscles of his torso, although somewhat thickened about the midriff, bore testament to his daily training in martial skills.

I myself had trained daily when younger, before I became a haizda mage. But now my hunting kept me fit and I preferred to rely on my instincts in battle rather than follow the routines of a High Mage.

It might be that Nunc was some way past his prime, but he would still be dangerous and I was aware that my ordeal in the water had taken its toll on my own stamina. Thus I could not endure a long struggle here. To win, I must finish Nunc off quickly.

With my left hand I undid the top three buttons of my coat and reached inside, withdrawing a short blade. Now, brandishing two blades, I moved round the desk and began to advance slowly towards the mage.

Out of the corner of my eye, I saw Nessa running towards Susan. I thought that she was rushing to comfort her sister, but then, to my astonishment, she picked up the spear that lay on the floor and charged straight at Nunc.

As the spear shattered against his shield, he used the latter like a club, swinging it sideways against the girl. It struck her on the shoulder and sent her flying into the panelled wall.

I saw my advantage. Nunc had made the mistake that would kill him. Taking the opportunity presented by Nessa's wild charge, I had followed close and swift upon her heels, and now, with a sweep of my sabre, I cut Nunc's throat.

Seeing my approach, he had tried to bring the shield back across to cover his body, but he was too late. Such was the speed and force of my blow that his head was almost severed. As he fell to the stone flags, I put my own sabre and dagger aside and sank onto my knees beside the dying High Mage.

I must feed. His blood represented strength. It promised a chance to escape from the fortress.

As the blood pumped from Nunc's neck, I fed greedily, drinking down the hot sweet blood in huge gulps, feeling the life-force filling my body with new strength.

THE SHAIKSA ASSASSIN

When I'd finished, I stood up and belched loudly. Better out than in!

By now Nessa was back on her feet, holding her shoulder and grimacing with pain. I had been impressed by her bravery – her actions had made it easier for me to defeat Nunc. Her face was pale and I could see her trembling, but apart from a little bruising she would no doubt make a full recovery. Purrai were very resilient. I smiled at her, but she just stared back, an expression of horror and revulsion on her face. So I licked my lips, went back into the bath house and knelt down beside the water. I bent over until I was almost touching its steaming surface, then, with both hands, began to sluice the blood off my face and hair.

As I finished, Nessa and Susan, arm in arm, came into the chamber behind me. I turned to face the two sisters and smiled again. But they looked at me as if I had done them harm rather than saving them from certain death. Of course, I had to make allowances for their condition. In addition to her damaged shoulder, one side of Nessa's face was badly grazed. She must have hurt it when Nunc dashed her aside with his shield. And Susan was extremely pale; she had been drained almost to the point of death.

'I'll get clothes for both of you,' I said. 'Sensible purrai clothes to keep you alive in the blizzard. Then we'll leave this place.'

Susan opened her mouth but no words came out. She was shaking all over after her experience with Nunc. But Nessa looked angry and determined.

'What about Bryony?' she demanded.

'Of course, Nessa, I'll get clothes for her too. But now we must escape this fortress. If you are to have any hope of life, you will do exactly what I say.'

I saw no point in upsetting her by revealing that Bryony was probably already dead. She would find out soon enough.

I led the way down the stone steps. Before me, I held out the sabre and a short blade; behind me, my tail stood up, quivering as it searched ahead for the slightest threat.

I seized garments for the two girls from a room used to store the clothes of the tower's slaves: warm hempen trousers, thick woollen upper garments and a waterproof cape and hood such as were worn by purrai when they attended to their duties in the inner courtyard. Carrying these, I continued the descent.

I hadn't bothered to collect any clothes for little Bryony – there were none small enough anyway – but Nessa accepted the big bundle I thrust into her arms without suspecting anything.

At last we came to the three rooms. The keys were back in the locks, but all the doors were wide open. I paused as, with a cry, Nessa rushed into all three rooms, one after the other, in search of her sister. Finally, her eyes wild with grief, she stormed up to me.

'Where is she? Where've they taken her?'

'Best to forget her, little Nessa. She'll be at peace now.'

'She's just a child!' Nessa cried, her face very close to mine. 'You promised that she'd be safe!'

'Forget her. We have to leave now. We must leave or we'll all die. If you still want to live, follow me now. Soon it will be too late.'

'I won't go without her.'

She was testing my patience. 'Then you'll die here, little Nessa. You'll change your mind when you feel the blades cut your flesh. They'll kill you very slowly . . .'

'I saved your life,' Nessa said, her voice almost a whisper. Then she reached forward and wrapped her fingers in my hair, pulling me down towards her until our foreheads were actually touching. 'You owe me a life. I saved you so you could save my sisters.'

I felt very strange. Her words shouldn't have been

disturbing, but they were. They spoke a truth that I couldn't deny, but they shouldn't have had even the slightest power over me. It was odd too to have her so close, to feel her fingers twisting in my hair.

In a strange way I liked it. I also liked the way her forehead was touching mine. No human had ever come so close to me before. No human had ever dared. Most would have put as much distance as possible between them and me. Yet here was this girl holding my head against hers and staring deep into my eyes.

With a sudden jerk, Nessa released me and stepped back, burying her face in her hands.

For a moment I could not think clearly. Then I heard myself speaking, and my voice seemed to come from a great distance; it was as though it belonged to another.

'Go and get our horses from the stables. Saddle them but leave the cart – the snow will be too deep by now. If your sister lives, I'll bring her to the outer gate. If I don't appear by the time you've finished readying the horses, ride off without me and head south. The weather will change within two days or less and I will catch you up.'

Then I led the sisters to the door that gave access to the large inner courtyard. When I opened it, snow was still whirling downwards. In the distance I saw the stables, the yellow lantern-light from within reflecting on the wet flags. I turned and thrust the short blade into Nessa's hand.

'If any purrai try to stop you, threaten them with this. They fear the blade more than anything – they grow up familiar with its bite. It is the chief means by which they are trained.'

Nessa nodded, determined, and went out into the snow with her sister following. She looked back once and I saw her eyes glitter in the darkness like two distant stars. Once again, I was astonished by what I was doing, astonished by my response to this purra.

From my previous visit here I knew the layout of the tower. The large cellar was used for feasts, and I went down the steps until I came to the stout oaken door. It was not locked. Those within did not fear intruders. I only needed to turn the huge iron ring at its centre and push it open.

I gripped the sabre firmly in my right hand and thrust my tail high up my back, searching beyond the door. First, I found the child. To my surprise, she still lived, but in moments that would change. They were preparing to cut her throat.

I began to assess the level of opposition. Some of those within were cooks; others were armourers or general labourers. Yet that still left thirty-nine hardy, well-trained warriors. I would be facing powerful odds.

Although I never doubted for a moment that I would be victorious, my chances of getting the child out in one piece were not good: in the heat of battle, all things are uncertain.

With my left hand, I slowly turned the ring to the right. Then, equally slowly, I gave the door a little push so that it opened gradually, creaking on its ancient hinges as it did so.

A large open fireplace was the focal point of the huge room; it was set within the far wall so that almost all the occupants –

Kobalos warriors and servants – were facing towards it with their backs to me. The room hummed with animated conversation. Several long tables stood between door and fireplace; they were heaped with dishes and tankards, but although there was some food on the plates, the main activity so far had clearly involved drinking a good deal of strong ale. Alcohol dulls the senses – a haizda mage would never defile his body in such a way. Their foolishness pleased me, lowering the odds against me.

The main course was yet to be served. Indeed, it had yet to be cooked. The spit did not currently hold meat, but it would not have long to wait, for Bryony had been forced to her knees close to the fire; a wooden bucket had been placed directly under her head to catch the blood. They had blindfolded the sobbing purra so she couldn't see what was about to happen to her – more out of expediency than mercy: even as I watched, a blade was being sharpened, ready to slit her throat. And then I saw her executioner and noted the three long, black, braided pigtails that marked him as a particularly dangerous adversary. Those three distinctive plaits showed that he was one of the *Shaiksa*, a brotherhood of elite assassins that answered only to the Triumvirate of High Mages who ruled Valkarky.

This made saving the child a much more difficult task.

The creak of the door was lost amidst the hubbub of many voices, but I quickly amplified it so that it filled the room with thunder, and all without exception turned to gaze at the source of that strange noise.

I stepped boldly forward into the room and called out in a loud challenging voice so that none could fail to hear my words or understand what it was that I said.

'Give the child to me!' I demanded. 'She is my lawful property and has been taken from me against my wishes and against all customs of hospitality and rights of ownership.'

CHAPTER
7
THE BITE OF A BLADE

⟡NESSA⟡

I led my sister, shivering with cold and fear, towards the stables. The wind was driving snowflakes into our faces but the flags were wet and steaming.

'How could you touch him, Nessa?' Susan asked. 'How could you bear to be so close to him?'

'I did what was necessary to save Bryony,' I replied.

In truth, I couldn't believe what I had just done – gripping him by the hair like that and dragging him close so that our foreheads were touching . . . He might have slain me on the spot. I had done it on the spur of the moment, driven to such recklessness by my fear for my little sister.

Somehow it had worked and I had survived the encounter.

Since Mother had died giving birth to her, Bryony had been like my own child. I *had* to save her.

There were two doors giving access to the stables, and as we reached the nearer one, Susan started to whimper with fear. I turned angrily and shushed her. I immediately felt guilty at doing so. I had behaved exactly as the beast would have done. But if any of the Kobalos heard us, we would die here. I thought of poor Bryony and hoped against hope that Slither would be in time to save her. Cautiously I moved into the area of yellow light cast by the lanterns and peered into the stables. The air was much warmer here, and smelled of hay and horse dung.

There were thirty or more stalls, all of them occupied. I began to walk slowly forward, peering into each one, looking for our own animals. I wasn't sure if I'd entered by the door we'd used before. Perhaps they were at the other end of the block? I strode purposefully forward.

Then two things happened that brought me to a halt. I heard harsh, guttural voices from the far end of the stables. There was nobody in sight, and I couldn't make out what they were saying, but they sounded like Kobalos. Next I became aware of something else: the first five or six horses were already saddled, each draped with two small bags of what looked like provisions. Why not take these and avoid the delay and risk of finding and saddling our own horses? I said to myself.

Quickly I pulled back the door of the stall and, seizing the bridle, led the first of the horses out. 'Take this one!' I said, passing it over to Susan.

'What about the cart and our trunks?' she complained. 'All my best clothes are inside.'

'We haven't time to get them, Susan. Our lives are at risk,' I snapped, turning my back on her.

It was the work of just a few moments to lead out two more horses – piebald like the first – from their stalls. I was just about to get a fourth mount when I heard someone crossing the wet flags and approaching the stable door behind us.

My heart began to pound in my chest. I was terrified. What if it was another of the fierce Kobalos like the beast who had attacked Susan? What chance would I have against something like that? For a moment I panicked completely and was ready to run and save myself. Then, with a sense of shame, I thought of Susan and Bryony. How could I leave them?

So I took a deep breath to steady myself, turned, and gripped the knife in my belt more tightly.

To my surprise, coming towards me was one of the fierce women who had taken me up to the bath house where I'd found Slither. She was carrying a club and I saw anger and purpose in her eyes. With a trembling hand I tugged the knife from my belt and pointed it towards her. The sight of it brought her to a stop about five paces short of me.

I feared the club she wielded, but I could see that my blade scared her more. I took a step towards her as if I meant to attack; she took a step as well – backwards, away from me.

'Susan, take the horses outside!' I shouted, keeping myself between the slave woman and my sister.

Twice Susan fumbled with the reins but managed to lead

the three piebald mares out into the yard. I followed, backing slowly and warily, never taking my eyes off the woman who held the cudgel. Now she was matching me step for step and I thought I saw a new determination in her eyes.

Her face was criss-crossed with scars, as were her arms. A slave's rearing and training were effected with the bite of a blade – so Slither had told me. No doubt I would face the same when I became a slave myself.

I tried a new tactic. 'Why don't you come with us?' I suggested, forcing a smile onto my face. 'You don't have to stay here and be mistreated. Escape with us!'

She did not reply, answering my words with a scowl. Suddenly I understood. If she allowed me to escape with the horses, she would be punished – perhaps even killed. She feared her masters more than she did me. But now I was out in the yard, and I had to protect my family.

'The gate! Lead them to the gate!' I shouted at Susan, pointing towards it.

The slave was still matching me step for step but had not yet attacked. Then I heard more female voices. Other slaves were running towards us – including their leader, the woman with the torch.

'I don't want to die! I don't want to die here!' Susan screamed. 'What did we do to deserve this? I wish I were back at the farm!'

I knew that it was all over now: Susan was correct – we would probably die here. But I had no intention of betraying my own terror and despair. Why give them the satisfaction?

I raised the blade to show that I would not go down without a fight.

The woman with the club held it aloft and ran straight towards me. I was scared but desperate, and as she brought down the club, intending to brain me, I slashed at her arm with the dagger.

The blade cut into her forearm. She screamed and the club dropped from her hand. Now she was looking at me with pain-filled eyes, while blood dripped from her arm onto the flags. For a moment it halted the others in their tracks. But then they began to move forward again.

Where was Slither? I wondered. Had he managed to rescue poor Bryony?

CHAPTER 8
ONLY ONE CHANCE

Thirty-nine Kobalos warriors faced me in the cellar. Thirty-nine warriors between me and the human child I had come to claim. They wore armour but were without helmets, as was customary on such occasions. The hair on their faces was long and obscured their mouths.

Then there was that most dangerous opponent: the pigtailed Shaiksa assassin who now held a blade to Bryony's throat.

For a moment the room became almost totally silent; all that could be heard was the crackling of the logs in the fireplace. Then, with a roar of anger, a warrior charged towards me, lifting a huge double-edged sword, ready for the kill.

I gave no ground, moving only at the very last second. I

stepped to the right, ducked under the descending blade and struck out sideways with my sabre. My blade bit into his neck and severed the spinal column so that my would-be killer fell stone dead at my feet.

Then I slowly flexed the fingers of my left hand so that the knuckles cracked, and then, with a wide, cruel smile, reached into my coat and withdrew my second blade, a dagger, so that now I faced my enemies with a sharp weapon in each hand.

'Give me what is rightfully mine. Give me what I demand. Do it quickly and I may let some of you live!' I shouted, amplifying my voice so that the dishes rattled and the knives and forks danced on the table-tops.

I had used those words as a distraction – because immediately, without waiting for a reply, I leaped up onto the nearest table. Then I was racing across the table-tops towards the fireplace, scattering silver dishes and golden goblets with my feet, all my will directed towards one end: to prevent the assassin crouching over the child from slaying her.

To control the assassin while dashing through my enemies was not easy. Shaiksa assassins are trained in a multitude of mind disciplines and can sometimes resist even the will of a mage.

Thus, even as I jumped down from the final table, he began to slice the blade up towards the child's throat. The blindfold had fallen from her eyes, and she shrieked as it approached her. But I struck out with the hilt of my own blade, driving it hard into the temple of my opponent so that he fell backwards, stunned, the weapon falling from his hand.

It did not pay to kill such a being wantonly. The Shaiksa never forget, and even as one lay close to death, his dying mind could reach out over a great distance to tell his brothers the name and location of his slayer. So it was pragmatism, not mercy, that had guided my hand.

I snatched up the child. She screamed as I lifted her, but I used the mage skill called *boska*: adjusting the chemical composition of the air in my lungs, I breathed quickly into her face and she fell instantly into a deep coma.

Then I turned back to face my enemies, who were approaching me with weapons drawn, faces filled with fury. I began to increase my size, simultaneously using my will to hurl into their faces a twitching pulse of naked fear so that, as I grew, their eyes rolled in their sockets and their mouths opened in dismay.

Then, with one final effort of will, I reached out with my mind and extinguished the thirteen torches that lit the subterranean banquet hall. It was instantly plunged into darkness, but through my mage eyes I could still see: for me, the room was lit by a silver spectral light. Thus I was able to escape the melee, passing safely through my enemies.

I had almost reached the door when I sensed a threat behind me. It was the Shaiksa assassin. He had recovered quickly and, unlike the warriors, was resisting my magic. Now he was racing towards me, twirling a blade in his left hand and a war-axe in his right. Every fibre of his being was focused upon slaying me.

Had it been possible, I would have stopped him using minimal force. In combat, one usually has options to choose from in order to counter an attack. But such was the ferocity of his assault and his determination to end my life that I had only one chance and was forced to employ it to save myself.

I ducked below his first blade, but I knew that I could not escape the second: this was arcing downwards towards my head, threatening to sever it from my neck. So I pierced the assassin's heart with my own blade. The effect was instantaneous – the axe dropped from his nerveless fingers, reaching the ground fractionally before his dead body.

With this victory I had saved my life, but I had changed it for ever. In killing the High Mage, I had made myself an outlaw in the eyes of the Triumvirate; but in killing the assassin I had directed the wrath of his brotherhood onto my head. They would seek vengeance and hunt me to the ends of the earth until I too was dead.

I ran into the yard not a moment too soon. Nessa and Susan had brought three horses out of the stables. Nessa was holding a knife uncertainly, trying to ward off four purrai who were converging on her. Susan was screaming hysterically.

But then I noted a fifth slave. She was cradling her arm, which was bleeding profusely. So Nessa had shown some courage and got at least one blow in! Another few moments, however, and it would have been all over. I ran towards them, and the other purrai shrieked and fled back towards the stables.

I glanced quickly at the three piebald mares – none were the mounts we had brought with us to the tower. In one respect that was good because these were shod in the Kobalos way, with wide shoes that afforded a better grip and prevented them from sinking into all but the very softest fresh snow. The rest was bad – very bad. All were saddled but they lacked saddle-bags and provisions. There was no grain for the horses. All they carried was the customary two small sacks of *oscher*, which could be used as emergency food for them. It was made of oats with special chemical additives that could sustain a beast of burden for the duration of a long journey. Of course, afterwards the horse would die and oscher was therefore only used as a last expedient. But what choice had Nessa given me?

With a curse, I leaped up onto the back of the nearest horse and draped the unconscious form of the child over the pommel.

'Thank God!' Nessa cried, but even now warriors might be running to lower the portcullis in order to prevent our escape from the courtyard. I pointed towards the gateway and urged my horse across the wet flags towards it. Nessa struggled to push her still-sobbing sister up onto one horse, then quickly mounted the other. Within moments, we were through the open gate and galloping down the cinder path into the whirling snowflakes.

For a while we rode in silence, save for Susan's infernal sobs, while I thought over the consequences of what I'd just done.

'Why are we heading north?' Nessa called out at last.

I did not bother to reply. Heading north was the only chance of life I had. And it was a slim chance at that. I had just two remaining options. The first was to become a fugitive, fleeing my enemies for as long as I was able. The other was to journey straight to the source of the danger and confront it – to head for Valkarky.

CHAPTER 9
NORTH TO VALKARKY

I guided us north towards the best chance of survival that remained. In two hours we reached the ruins of a farmhouse. It was very old and had been overrun when the climate had changed more than two millennia earlier. At that time my people had pushed their boundaries further south, meeting little opposition from the small, weak kingdoms of divided humans.

Now all that remained of it was two stark stone walls in the lee of a steep hillside. As I approached the ruin I sensed something, an unseen malevolence. I halted, prompting Nessa to ask, 'Why do we stop? We must get inside!' But I ignored her and raised my tail to search for the source of my unease. As I did so, a shower of small stones began to fall onto my shoulders and head.

In a moment I had found it. It was a bychon, a spirit able to manipulate matter. Some were very dangerous and could hurl large boulders with great accuracy to crush a victim, but this one seemed relatively weak. I nudged it with my mind and it retreated to a dark corner. Then I whispered to it so that the purrai behind could not hear my words:

'Soon we will be gone from here and then you may reclaim this place as your home. Do not behave in a way that will force me to drive you out permanently. Be still and keep hidden. Do you accept my offer?'

No more pebbles fell around me, so I took the bychon's silence as acceptance of my offer. I immediately made good use of the old wood that lay scattered about the site. First I constructed a lean-to to provide some shelter against the blizzard. Some of the remaining wood I ignited by force of will – a fire to provide life-giving warmth.

In their sensible purrai clothes, the two older girls were quite well protected, but when I had snatched the child, she'd been readied for the blade and was almost naked. My use of boska had placed her in a deep coma, but it was dangerous to keep her in that condition too long. Thus I was forced to awaken her, whereupon she immediately began to shiver and cry weakly and I knew that she lacked the strength to survive for long.

I am comfortable even in the coldest of temperatures so I could manage without my long black coat. However, it was not for warmth that I wore this garment; it was a mark of my vocation and status as a haizda mage, its thirteen buttons representing the thirteen truths that it has taken me many years of study to learn. I was reluctant to remove it, but I knew that the child would soon die without its protective warmth and felt bound by my trade with Old Rowler. So I took it off and wrapped her in it, handing her to Nessa, who then crouched with her close to the fire, whispering softly to her in reassurance.

'Little Nessa,' I asked gently, 'where are our saddlebags? Where is the food that will keep us alive?'

Nessa hung her head. 'I was afraid,' she said. 'We just took the first horses we saw. I could hear Kobalos voices at the far end of the stables. Then those fierce women interrupted us – I threatened them with the blade and cut one, but they kept creeping closer. My sister was weeping with fear. I thought I acted in our best interests.'

I could see that she was troubled by her actions. 'Then I will do what I can,' I said. 'Do you still have my blade?'

Nessa nodded and withdrew it from beneath her cape, handing it to me handle foremost. I accepted it with the hint of a smile and readied myself for what had to be done.

I removed my boots and, wearing just the thin diagonal belt with the scabbards securing the two short blades, trudged up the hill into the teeth of the blizzard. In truth, I enjoyed the conditions; for a Kobalos, such a storm was exhilarating.

Soon I reached a large plateau, an area of high moorland, and there dropped to all fours and began to run swiftly with my tail arched high above my back, seeking for likely prey.

Little moved in that blizzard. Distantly, I sensed arctic foxes and rodents and a few hardy birds, but all were too distant. It was then that I came upon the wolves.

It was a large pack, heading south with the storm wind. They would have passed by me at least three leagues to the west, but I exerted my will and summoned them; they hurried towards me, scenting easy prey. To give them more encouragement, I turned and began to flee before them, loping easily across the snow.

Only when they were almost upon me did I increase my speed. Faster and faster I ran, until only the leader of the pack, a huge white wolf – sleek, heavily muscled and in its prime – could keep me in sight. Together we drew away from the remainder who, without their leader, soon tired of the chase and were left far behind, wandered aimlessly, howling up at the invisible moon.

When the wolf was almost upon me, I turned to meet it. We both charged, fur against fur, teeth snarling, to roll over and over in the deep snow, gripping each other in a death-lock. The wolf bit deep into my shoulder, but to me the pain was nothing; with my own teeth, I savaged its throat, tearing away the flesh so that its blood spurted forth bright red upon the white snow.

I drank deeply while the huge animal twitched beneath me in its death throes. Not a drop of the hot sweet thick blood did I waste. When my thirst was sated, I drew a blade and cut off the beast's head, tail and legs and, walking upright, carried its body across my shoulders, back to the ruin of the farmhouse.

Close to the fire, while the girls watched with wide eyes, I skinned and gutted the wolf, then cut it into small pieces and buried them in the hot embers to cook.

All three sisters ate their fill that night, and only Susan complained, whimpering as she struggled to chew the half-burned, half-cooked meat. But she was quickly silenced by Nessa, who understood that I had given them the hope of life.

Just before dawn I fed the fire with wood, and as I did so, Nessa awoke. She came to sit opposite me so that our eyes locked across the flames. Strangely she didn't seem quite so skinny tonight. Her neck was particularly inviting and my mouth watered so that I was forced to swallow.

'I don't like it here,' she said. 'I keep getting a sense that something is watching us. I heard a noise too, like a small shower of falling stones. It could be a dangerous boggart. Perhaps this is its lair.'

'What is a boggart?' I demanded, filled with curiosity.

'It's a malevolent spirit. Some throw rocks or even big boulders. They are dangerous and can kill people.'

'How would you deal with such an entity?' I demanded.

'I wouldn't even try,' Nessa said. 'But far to the south across the sea it is rumoured that there are spooks – men who are capable of dealing with such things.'

From what she described, it was likely that 'boggart' was the human term for bychon. But in all my years of learning I had never heard of their spooks. I wondered what kind of magic they used.

'Well, worry not, little Nessa – a spook is not needed here. In dark places there are often invisible things that linger and watch. But you are safe with me.'

'How much longer before we can travel on?' she asked. 'And why are we going north?'

'Perhaps we'll be able to leave at dawn tomorrow, or by the afternoon at the latest,' I answered. 'But without grain the horses won't get far. There is oscher in the small sacks, which will give them strength for a little while – before it kills them. You'll be eating horseflesh before the week is out. It's easier to chew than wolf, so perhaps your sister will not complain so much. Eventually, in order to survive, we might have to eat one of your two sisters – Susan would be best because she's bigger, with more meat on her bones.'

Nessa gasped. 'How can you even think such a horrible thing?'

'Because it is better for one to die so that the others may live. It is the way of the Kobalos world, so you might as well get used to it, little Nessa.'

'What about your promise!' she exclaimed. 'You agreed to take my sisters to safety.'

'I did, and I will strive with all the powers at my command to keep to my trade with your poor father.'

Nessa was silent for a moment, but then she stared right into my eyes. 'If it proves necessary, eat me rather than one of my sisters.'

Once again I found myself surprised by her bravery – but, 'I will be unable to oblige,' I told her. 'You see, only you belong to me, and I would not waste my own chattel. Anyway, let us talk more of such things if the need arises. It'll be a long journey north. And I will now tell you why we are heading in that direction. We are going to Valkarky, where I must plead my case – it is the only hope of life I have. To save your little sisters I killed a High Mage, and an assassin whose brotherhood will seek vengeance and hunt me down until I am dead. But those I slew broke the law regarding my property rights. If I can successfully make my plea before the ruling Triumvirate, they will not be able to touch me.'

'What is Valkarky – another fortress?'

'No, Nessa, it is a city. Our city! It is the most beautiful and most dangerous place in this whole wide world,' I answered. 'Even a human such as you, with poor, half-blind eyes, cannot fail to appreciate its beauty. But never fear, I will protect you from its many dangers.'

'It would be better to die here,' Nessa said bitterly, 'than enter a city full of others like you.'

'Die? Die, little Nessa? Who said anything about dying? You gave me back my life, and in return I'll protect you and your two plump sisters, just as I promised. Only in extremis will we eat one of them, and then only so that the other might live. I have made a promise, but I can only do what is possible. If only you had got the horses with their provisions as I commanded!'

A look of embarrassment flashed across Nessa's face, but she was silent, evidently deep in thought. 'But you'll still take them to safety when your business is done?'

I smiled but refrained from showing my teeth. 'Of course. Haven't I promised as much? Now go back to sleep. What else is there for your kind to do but sleep when it snows so hard?'

'My father said that you also sleep in the depths of winter. He said that you hibernate. Why do you do that when you love the cold so much?'

I shrugged. 'A haizda mage sleeps in shudru, deepest winter, in order to learn. It is a time when he gathers his thoughts within deep dreams and weaves new knowledge out of experience. We dream to see the truth at the heart of life.'

Nessa turned away and looked back to where her sisters were sleeping. Bryony was still tightly wrapped within my coat – only her mousy brown hair was visible.

'What is Valkarky like?' Nessa asked, turning back to face me.

'It is vast,' I explained. 'We believe that our city will not stop growing until it covers the whole world. Not a rock, not a tree, not even a blade of grass will be visible then. All other cities will be crushed beneath its expanding walls!'

'That's horrible!' she cried. 'It's unnatural. You would make the whole world hideous.'

'You do not understand, little Nessa, so do not judge until you have seen it with your own eyes.'

'But it's a nonsense, anyway. How could a city become so large? There could not be enough builders to create such a monstrosity.'

'Valkarky's walls are constantly being constructed and repaired by creatures that need no sleep. They spit soft stone from their mouths, and this is used as building material. It resembles wood pulp at first, but hardens soon after contact with the air. Hence the name Valkarky – it means the City of the Petrified Tree. It is a wonderful place, full of entities created by magic – beings that can be seen in no other place. Be grateful that you will get to see it. All other humans who enter there are slaves or marked for death. You have some hope of leaving it.'

'You forget that I also am a slave,' Nessa replied angrily.

'Of course you are, little Nessa. But in exchange for your bondage, your two sisters will go free. Doesn't that make you happy?'

'I owe obedience to my father and I am willing to sacrifice my life so that my sisters will be safe. But it certainly does not make me happy. I was looking forward to my life, and now it has been taken away. Should I rejoice at that?'

I did not reply. Nessa's future, or lack of it, was not worth debating. I had not told her just how bad things were. The odds against me were indeed great, and I would probably be taken and killed, either on the journey or immediately upon entering the city. It was unlikely that I would live long enough to make a successful plea to the ruling council. If I died, the three girls would become slaves at best; at worst they would be drained of blood and eaten.

After that Nessa became very quiet; she went off to sleep without even wishing me a good night. Humans such as Nessa often lack manners, so I wasn't really surprised.

About an hour after dawn, the wind dropped and the blizzard became just a light whirling of snowflakes falling lazily out of the grey dome of the sky.

'I need my coat back, little Nessa,' I told her. 'You will have to share what you have with your youngest sister.'

Sooner or later I would have to fight, and I wanted to be wearing the long black coat, my badge of office, so that any enemy would appreciate the strength of what he faced. I noted that it was Nessa who surrendered some of her garments to clothe the child, including her waterproof cape. They were far too big but would provide the necessary protection against the elements. Nessa would now find the conditions more difficult. I noted that Susan did not volunteer any of her garments.

As was my custom, before mounting my horse I stood in front of it and breathed quickly into its nostrils three times.

'What are you doing?' Nessa asked, her face alive with curiosity. She had obviously wisely decided not to fight against my wishes.

'I am using what we mages call *boska*. I have changed the composition of the air within my lungs before breathing into its nostrils. I have thus infused the animal with obedience and courage. Now, if I have to fight, my mount will not flinch from the enemy that faces us!'

'Will you have to fight? Does danger threaten?' she asked.

'Yes, little Nessa, it is very likely. So now we must press on and hope for the best.'

'How much further have we to travel? Each day seems the same. I'm losing track of time – it seems like weeks have passed already.'

'This is merely our fifth morning. It is better not to think about the rest of the journey. Just take each day as it comes.'

We left the old farmhouse behind. Soon we came to a rocky, barren area where the snow had melted. Steam rose from cracks in the ground, and from time to time the earth trembled and there was a smell of burning on the breeze.

'What's this place?' Nessa asked, riding up alongside me.

'It is the Fittzanda Fissure, an area of earthquakes and in-stability. This is the southern boundary of our territories. Soon we will be in the land of my people.'

We continued north across that steaming, shaking terrain, our horses even more nervous than the three purrai. The area was vast, and its shifting rocky nature would make us difficult to track. Those who pursued us from the fortress would expect me to flee south – not north to what might well be my execution – so that was to my advantage.

And soon others would be hunting us too. The dying thoughts of the assassin would have been sent out to his brotherhood. They would know who had slain him. Some would already be out there in the snowy wilderness or even close by, and they would sense my location and begin to converge on our path. The Triumvirate of High Mages might also send further assassins from Valkarky.

Out here they would try to kill me on sight. I needed to reach the city in one piece in order to win the right of plea before the council.

Only one thing bothered me. Did I still have the courage and ruthlessness to defeat my enemies? Or had I already been infected with skaiium, as my softness towards Nessa indicated?

It was not long before an enemy found me – but it was not the Shaiksa assassin I'd expected. The High Mages had sent a very different creature.

The assassin waited directly ahead of us. At first glance it appeared to be an armed Kobalos on horseback, but there was something wrong where the rider and horse joined. It was not simply that there was no saddle. There was no division between them. I was not looking at two creatures; it was one deadly composite.

'What is that fearsome thing?' Nessa demanded with a shudder. Susan began to whimper, while Bryony shook with terror but made no sound.

'Perhaps it is our deaths,' I told her. 'Stay back and let me do what I can.'

I was facing a hyb warrior, a crossbreed of Kobalos and horse that had been designed for combat. The creature's upper body was hairy and muscular, combining exceptional strength with speed and the ability to rip an opponent to pieces. The hands were also specially adapted for fighting. In its right the hyb appeared to be gripping five long, thin blades, but I knew they were talons that could be retracted into the muscular hand or unsheathed at will. In its left was a mace – a huge club covered in sharp spikes like the quills of a porcupine.

The lower body of a hyb was faster than a horse, with spurs of bone projecting from each foreleg, often used to disembowel the mount of its enemy. Additionally, this hyb was armoured: it wore a metal helmet that covered its whole face except for the angry red eyes. Its body, upper and lower, was also protected by the highest quality ribbed armour.

The helmet, with its elongated jaw, betrayed the true shape of the upper head, which was more horse than Kobalos. Both mouths were open now, snorting clouds of steam into the cold air. Then both throats called out a challenge, a deep guttural roar that echoed across the land from horizon to horizon. Without further ado it charged towards me, through a narrow gap between two jets of steam erupting from the volcanic rock.

I heard whinnies of fear from behind as the two purrai

mounts, sensing the strangeness and malevolence of the hyb, scattered, taking their riders with them. But my horse, fortified as it was by the magic of boska, did not move a muscle.

The hyb whirled the club high above its head, but I saw through that subterfuge. It was intended to distract me, and while I looked up, the long thin talons would strike fast and low like vipers' tongues.

It was as I anticipated, and I was ready. I charged forward to meet the attack, tail extended, and we passed each other with barely a foot between us. As the hyb leaned towards me, the sharp tips of its talons aimed upwards, seeking to slip beneath my ribs and into my heart, I focused my mind until a small bright magical shield materialized in the air and moved with me.

I positioned it so that it deflected the five deadly talons. I did not immediately strike a blow of my own but, guiding my mount with my knees, drew my sabre and followed up my advantage, catching the creature before it had fully come about.

I struck it full upon the head with the hilt of my sabre so that the metal of the helmet rang. Then, with my dagger, I tried to pierce its neck at the point of relative weakness where the helmet joined the body armour.

I failed, and we broke contact, both galloping some distance apart.

Quickly, the hyb turned and charged for the second time. This time, however, despite its agility and speed, I was even better prepared and, while deflecting the talons with my shield for a second time, struck a blow of my own.

I did not have the space to put all my strength into the scything horizontal sweep of my blade, but luck was with me.

The moment I struck, a jet of steam erupted from the ground almost immediately under my enemy. The horse screamed with pain and the upper part leaned towards me to avoid being scalded. Thus the hyb was distracted, and my sabre made contact high on the shoulder; deflected by the ribbed armour there, it found the narrow gap between the helmet and the shoulder piece, biting into the neck so that the hyb rocked sideways as it passed.

As the creature swayed and the mace dropped from its nerveless fingers, I drove my magical shield towards it like a hammer; the blow was terrible and it fell sideways, its four legs buckling beneath it. It hit the ground with a heavy thud, rolled over in the snow and lay still.

I dismounted and approached my enemy with caution. I had expected the hyb assassin to be more difficult to defeat and half expected some trick. I glanced at its lower body and saw the assortment of blades and weapons in sheaths on its flanks.

It was now at my mercy, so I pulled off its helmet and held a blade at its throat.

The hyb was unconscious, its eyes tight shut. I had no time to waste, so I sent a magical barb straight into its brain so that it awoke with a scream. The eyes suddenly opened wide and gleamed a malevolent red. For a moment I felt giddy, and the world seemed to spin; my grip loosened upon my blade. *What was wrong with me?* I wondered.

Just in time I became aware of the danger from the creature's eyes. I could barely look away, the compulsion to stare into them was so strong; they had an hypnotic quality, and had the power to suck away the will so that time ceased to matter.

I regained my focus and stared instead at its mouth, which was full of big teeth. I spoke slowly in case the creature was still befuddled from that last terrible blow I had struck. 'Listen very carefully to me,' I warned it, pressing the knife into its throat so that I drew forth just a little blood. 'I have been wronged and I go to make my plea before the Triumvirate in Valkarky. It is my right.'

'You have no rights, mage!' the hyb roared, spitting the words up into my face, its big horse-teeth gnashing together. 'You have murdered one of the High Mages and are to be killed on sight!'

'He attempted to obstruct me when I was in the lawful process of repossessing my property. It was a criminal act and he attacked me further. In self-defence I was forced to kill him. But I have no personal quarrel, either with you or with any other High Mages. Give me your word that you will not oppose me further and I will set you free. Then you may bear witness to my plea in Valkarky and oppose it if you wish.'

'You are dead, mage, whether by my hand or another's. The moment you set me free I will cut your flesh and drink your blood.'

'Your fighting days are over,' I said, looking down at the creature. 'It is I who will wield a blade. It is for me to cut and for you to bleed. Soon I will drink *your* blood. It is as simple as that. There is only pain left for you now.'

There were screams as I killed it. Not one came from the hyb; the creature died bravely, as I had expected. It could do no less. The screams came from Nessa and her sisters, who had brought their mounts under control and returned when they saw that the danger had passed. It was almost an hour before Bryony stopped sobbing.

After telling the girls to control themselves, I led them on in silence. I thought over my fight with the hyb. What had gone wrong for the creature? Perhaps it had underestimated my capabilities – or maybe luck had played a part?

I realized that was certainly true. The jet of steam had surprised it and given me an advantage. This detracted from the feelings of pride I should have felt with the defeat of such a powerful adversary. I was not safe from skaiium yet. I must strive even harder to avoid its clutches and maintain my strength as a warrior mage.

The three purrai avoided my gaze and wore expressions of revulsion on their faces. Could they not understand that it had been necessary to kill, and that by doing so I had preserved all our lives?

That night I found us a cave to shelter in. There was no wood to use for fuel so we could only chew on the remaining strips of meat that I had cut from the wolf the day before.

'This is no life at all!' Susan complained. 'Oh, I wish Father still lived, and this was just a nightmare, and I could wake up safe and warm in my own bed!'

'We cannot change what's been done,' Nessa told her. 'Try to be brave, Susan. Hopefully, in a few weeks you'll start a new life. Then all this will seem just like a bad dream.'

Nessa spoke confidently as she put her arm round Susan to comfort her, but I noted the sadness in her own eyes. *Her* new life would be one of slavery.

After a while, I left the sisters alone to console each other and went to sit in front of the cave, gazing up at the stars. It was a very bright, clear night, and all five thousand of them were visible – amongst them the red, bloodshot eye of Cougis, the Dog Star, which was always my favourite.

Suddenly there was a streak of light in the northern sky, passing quickly from east to west. I estimated that it was somewhere over Valkarky. There was a superstition that such a falling star presaged a death or overthrow of some mage. Others in a position of danger would have taken that as a portent of their own demise, but I do not subscribe to such foolishness, so I thrust the thought from my mind and began to focus my will.

I was meditating, attempting to strengthen my mind against the possible onset of skaiium, when Nessa emerged from the cave and sat down beside me. She was wrapped in a blanket but was shivering violently.

'You should stay in the cave, little Nessa. It is too cold out here for a poor weak human.'

'It is cold,' she agreed, her voice hardly more than a whisper, 'but it's not just that making me shiver. How could you? How could you do that in front of me and my sisters?'

'Do what?' I asked. I wondered if I had been chewing the

wolf-meat too noisily. Maybe I had inadvertently burped or passed wind.

'The way you killed that creature and drank its blood – it was horrible. Even worse than what you did in the tower. And you delighted in it!'

'I must be honest with you, little Nessa, and tell you that, yes, it was most enjoyable to triumph over a deadly hyb warrior. I have killed a High Mage, a Shaiksa assassin and a hyb warrior over the past days – few of my people are able to boast of such an achievement!

'I offered him his freedom, but he refused, and would have continued his attempt against my life – and then yours and your sisters'. So what was I supposed to do? I must confess that his blood did taste sweet and I must apologize if I slurped it too greedily. But otherwise I behaved quite properly.'

'Properly?!' cried Nessa. 'It was monstrous! And now you are taking us to a city populated by many thousands of beings such as yourself!'

'No, you are wrong,' I told her. 'I am a haizda mage. There are probably no more than a dozen of us in existence at this time. We are not city people – we live on the extreme fringes of Kobalos territory. We farm humans and see that they are happy and content.'

'Farm! What do you mean you *farm* humans?'

'It is nothing to worry about, Nessa. Why do you find it so alarming? You, your father and your sisters were all part of my farm, which is called a haizda – thus I am termed a haizda mage. We harvest blood to sustain us – along with other materials that may be of use. Your dead father knew the true situation, but he did not wish to upset you. He made a trade with me so that I would keep my distance. You believed I was just a dangerous creature that lived nearby, but in truth I owned you.'

'What?!' Nessa raised a hand to her face in shock. 'You took the blood of my father and my sisters? My blood too?'

'I did so at first, but later chose not to continue. I respected your father and decided to trade rather than take. He supplied me with red wine and bullock blood, both of which I am quite partial to. We had an agreement that suited us both. But, yes, other humans in the haizda give me blood. But most do not know it is happening – I usually take it in the night when they are sleeping.

'I make myself very small and slither into their house through a tiny hole in a roof or wall. Then I blow myself up to a comfortable size and crawl onto their beds. I sit on the human's chest, lean forward and make a small puncture in the neck. Then I drain a little blood – never enough to affect their health too adversely. Just as a human farmer concerns himself with the health and welfare of his cattle, so I husband my resources. The worst they ever experience is a little night-terror – like a nightmare in which a demon has sat on their chest, making it difficult to breathe. Very rarely they feel slightly dizzy on first rising – mostly the ones who leap out of bed too quickly. The puncture marks on the neck heal very quickly and, by first light, are easily mistaken for insect bites. Most humans on a farm are quite unaware of what is going on.'

Nessa had fallen silent, and when I glanced at her, I saw that she was staring at me, eyes wide. It was a long time before she spoke.

'You said "other materials". What else do you take?'

'Souls, little Nessa. Sometimes I use the souls of your people.'

She looked back to the cave, presumably to check that her sisters were still sleeping, before she spoke. 'How can you "use" a soul?' she managed eventually. 'That sounds horrible!'

'The owners don't mind because they are always dead before it happens. And dead souls are usually confused for quite a while before they find their way home. I just use up a little of their energy until they manage that. So really, I just borrow them.'

'Their "home" – where is that?'

'That depends. Some are an "Up" and others are a "Down". The first spin away into the sky silently; the others plunge into the ground, giving a sort of groan or sometimes a shriek or a howl – I don't know where *their* home is, but none of them seem very happy to be going there.'

'Were you present when my father died?'

'Yes, Nessa, I was. He took a long time to die and was in a lot of pain. It wasn't a pleasant death, and because you were so inconsiderate and ran off, he could have died all alone. But I was patient and stayed with him to the end.'

'Did you borrow his soul?'

'No, I wasn't given the chance. Some souls aren't confused at all. They don't linger but go home straight away.'

'Which way did my father go?'

'He was an "Up", little Nessa. So be happy for him. His soul sprang up into the sky without even the slightest of groans.'

'Thank you.' Nessa spoke quietly, and then she got to her feet and went back into the cave without another word.

Of course I'd lied about 'borrowing' souls. After you've taken their power there isn't really much of them left. Once released, they spin slowly for a few moments, then give a little whimper and fade away. So they never get to go home – that's the end of them. That might not be a bad thing with those who go down, but the others – the 'Ups' – might have lost a lot. It was a good thing for Old Rowler that he hadn't lingered.

CHAPTER 11
HIS BIG STINKY MOUTH

❧NESSA❧

I went back into the cave and waited for my eyes to adjust
to the darkness. In the dim flicker of the campfire, I made
out the forms of my two sisters. I could tell by their breathing that only Bryony was sleeping.

Saying nothing, I lay down, wrapped my blanket tightly
about me, and tried my best to sleep. But I was upset,
remembering over and over again the way Father had died,
unable to get it out of my head. I was so ashamed that I'd run
away and left him with just the beast for company.

Then another thought snared me. I couldn't stop thinking
about what Slither had said – how he harvested blood and

souls. Something slowly came into my mind. I remembered my dream – the recurrent nightmare I'd had as a child – and now, suddenly, it all made horrible sense. Over and over again I'd dreamed of being paralysed in bed, unable to call for help, while something terrible sat on my chest, making it hard to breathe, and sucked blood from my neck.

As I grew older the nightmare had become less frequent and had then faded away altogether. I had assumed that my glimpses of the beast through my bedroom curtains when he'd visited the farm had given rise to my nightmare. Now, at last, I knew the truth. It had been real. It could be no coincidence that my nightmares had ended soon after Father had started to trade with Slither. That must have been part of the on-going deal between the two of them – that Slither would leave us children alone.

Had part of that trade also been Father's promise that if anything ever happened to him, Slither could have me in exchange for the safety of Susan and Bryony? It was hard to accept the idea that I must sacrifice myself. Had my father truly loved me? I wondered.

I thrust my doubts aside. Of course he had. Hadn't he written that he would have sacrificed himself for us if necessary? Now I must do what I could to save my sisters.

'Oh, I'm scared, so scared!' Susan called out.

'Shhh!' I said. 'Keep your voice down or you'll wake Bryony.'

'What are we going to do?' Susan asked more quietly. 'He's taking us north to his own people. One is bad enough, but what about when we have to face hundreds or even thousands? They'll kill us and eat us. Have you seen the way the beast stares at me? He keeps looking at my neck. He can't wait to sink his teeth into me!'

She was right, but so far Slither had resisted his urges. 'He's savage, that's true enough,' I told her. 'But he is certainly a creature of his word. He promised our father that you and Bryony would be safe, and I have no reason to believe that he will not honour that. Hasn't he fought his own people to preserve us? We need to stay calm and believe that things will turn out for the best.'

I kept my own doubts to myself. It had been dangerous enough in the tower. How would we fare in Valkarky, where so many beasts might attack us?

'How can we ever be happy again now that Father is dead and we've left our home for ever? It's so cold, and it's getting worse with every mile we travel north. Will we ever be warm and comfortable?' Susan wailed, her voice rising with every word. 'We left our trunks behind in that awful tower and all my best clothes were inside. I'll never wear nice things again.'

Now she'd woken Bryony, who began to sob quietly. I suddenly felt very angry. Susan had always been selfish – no doubt that had come from being Father's favourite. I was the eldest, yet Susan had always been bought new clothes while I'd routinely been given her cast-offs – I'd had to take them in so they would fit. Even the dress I was wearing now had once belonged to Susan.

'You always think of yourself and nobody else!' I snapped.

'You've woken your sister and frightened her. You should be ashamed, Susan!'

Susan began to cry then, and that made Bryony worse.

Immediately I felt sorry for my outburst. We had to stick together while we still could. I knew it was harder, much harder, for Susan to adapt to this new situation. I had helped Father with the farm work – milking the cows, herding the sheep and feeding the chickens. I'd even taken his tools and repaired some of the fences. Mine had been mostly an outdoor life while Susan had made the beds and swept the floors. Of course she'd left the cooking and washing-up to me. So she'd had it relatively easy. No wonder she was finding our new life with the beast hard. I had to make allowances.

'Hush! Hush!' I called out more gently now. 'Come here, Bryony. Come and sit by me and I'll tell you a story.'

For a moment or two Bryony didn't reply, but then, dragging her blanket with her, she crawled across and sat next to me. I put my arms around her and gave her a hug.

'Tell me about the witches again, Nessa,' she begged.

Bryony loved tales about witches, and, sitting in front of the kitchen fire on a dark winter's evening, I had been only too happy to oblige. I'd told her the tales I'd learned from my mother. Bryony had never known her, so it pleased me to take her place and do what she'd have done if she'd lived. The witches I told her about were from Pendle, a place a long way to the south and in a foreign country far across a cold sea. She loved to hear about the different types of magic they used – some cutting off the thumb-bones of their enemies to steal their magical power. They were scary stories, but heard in a happy and secure environment. In those days Bryony knew nothing of Slither, and I'd ensured that when he visited the farm to talk to my father she never even glimpsed him.

But this was different. We were far from safe, and in the power of a creature who seemed just as dangerous as the witches I'd told Bryony about. I didn't think telling her that kind of story was a good idea now.

'I've got a different kind of story for you tonight, Bryony. It's a nice one about a handsome prince.'

'Oh, yes – that would be nice! Tell me a really nice story, Nessa,' she said. 'Tell me one where everything turns out happily in the end.'

The last thing I felt like was telling a story, but for her sake I did my best. 'Once upon a time an evil ogre carried off a princess and locked her in a tower—'

'What did the ogre look like?' Bryony interrupted.

'He was big and ugly,' I said, 'with one huge bulging blood-shot eye in the middle of his forehead. But news of the princess's captivity came to the attention of a prince, who saddled his horse and rode to the rescue—'

'Was the prince handsome?' Bryony demanded.

I was finding it hard to concentrate because I could hear the beast moving around outside; I wasn't much good at telling stories anyway. But at least I had her attention.

'Yes, he was tall, with fair hair and blue eyes, and he wore a sword with a silver hilt in a leather scabbard.'

'Did he have nice teeth and sweet breath?' Bryony asked.

'Yes, his breath was sweeter than spring blossom.'

'Better than the beast's breath then.' Susan spoke up now. 'It stinks of rotten meat and blood.'

'*Shhh!*' I hissed. 'He has sharp ears.'

'His teeth are really long and sharp too,' Bryony added.

I took a deep breath and tried to continue with the story, but Susan interrupted again. 'I'll tell the story this time, Nessa. *Your* stories are always so boring and predictable!'

I was too weary to protest so I let her carry on from where I'd left off.

'The handsome prince rode up to the dark tower,' she said, 'and he was lucky because the fierce ogre with long sharp teeth and breath smelling of blood and rotten meat wasn't at home. So the prince broke down the door and went up to the top of the tower and, after stealing one quick kiss from the beautiful princess, carried her down the steps and lifted her up onto his horse.'

Bryony had giggled when it came to the bit about the kiss and I began to relax.

'But the ogre had been hiding in the trees behind the tower, and he rushed out and attacked the prince, who drew his sword,' Susan continued.

'Did the handsome prince cut off the ogre's head?' Bryony asked, almost breathless with anticipation.

There was a pause. I should have seen it coming, but I didn't, and I was too late to intervene.

'No,' Susan said. 'The ogre opened his big stinky mouth and

bit off the head of the prince. Then he ate the horse and finished off the princess for his dessert!'

Bryony screamed and began to sob again, and at that moment the beast lurched into the cave.

'Be silent!' he growled. 'End this foolishness now. You will need all your strength in the morning!'

The fierce way he spoke stunned us all into silence. I lay there for a long time, listening and waiting for the breathing of my two sisters to change as they slipped into sleep. Above it all I could hear the harsh, heavy snoring of the beast. At last I fell asleep myself and began to dream.

The rat is crawling up onto my body now. I can feel its small sharp claws pricking into my skin through the blankets. It is sitting on my chest. Its tail goes thumpety-thump, *faster and faster, keeping perfect time with the beating of my heart.*

And now there is a new thing, even more terrifying. The rat seems to be growing heavier by the second. Its weight is pressing down on my chest, making it difficult to breathe. How can that be possible? How can a rat be so large and heavy?

CHAPTER
12
THE KEEPER OF THE GATE

The following day we made good progress, but finally it became necessary to kill one of the horses for food.

Despite her protests, I chose Nessa's mount because I judged it to be the weakest of the three. Of course, when I started to drink its hot sweet blood, the purrai became upset. That didn't stop them eating the meat once I'd cooked some for them, though. They did what I did in order to survive. So why did they turn from me in revulsion?

From then on, Nessa and Susan were forced to ride together while I carried the youngest purra with me. Nessa protested and offered to ride with me so that Bryony could be with her elder sister, but I refused. I might have to fight again at any moment so I wanted to spare my own horse as much as possible. Bryony was light, and mercifully she didn't make a fuss about riding with me, though I could feel that she held herself rigid with terror.

Finally, after another week of travelling, we were within sight of Valkarky. It was just after midday, and although at this latitude the sun was still low in the sky, it was a bright clear day and the visibility was excellent.

'What are those lights?' Nessa asked, bringing her horse alongside mine. She stared directly into my eyes as she spoke, but her sister clung to her back and averted her face so that she would not have to look at me.

On the horizon there was a shimmering curtain of colour, the whole spectrum of the rainbow. At times it seemed to open, giving a glimpse of what seemed to be utter blackness within.

'The lights shine from the eyes and mouths of the creatures who are building Valkarky,' I answered. 'Soon the walls of the city will be in view. That sight will delight your eyes and fill your hearts with happiness!'

I was proud of our city, but having chosen the vocation of a haizda mage, I lived far away in order to learn and develop my magic. Now, in truth, I was happy to be away from its intrigues and bustle, but it was still good to return occasionally to the place of my birth.

As we got closer, the three sisters found it difficult to look upon the city – it gleamed too brightly; nor could they appreciate the beauty of the industrious sixteen-legged *whoskor*, which swarmed over Valkarky's outskirts, engaged in the never-ending task of extending it. The eyes of these creatures swayed gracefully upon long black stalks and their brown fur rippled in the breeze as they spat soft stone from their mouths before working it skilfully with their delicate forelimbs, adding it to the new sections of wall.

We were approaching the southern edge of the developing city. Here the walls were uneven in height, obviously in various states of construction.

'Those are terrible creatures walking the walls!' Nessa cried, pointing up towards the whoskor. Bryony and Susan were wide-eyed and silent in their shock. 'They are so huge and there are so many of them. We can't go in there! We can't! Take us away, please.'

But I disregarded her protests and the wailing of her terrified sisters. We followed the road that led up to the main gate, flanked on either side by the walls. The further we travelled into the city, the older the fortifications. In the course of our journey, which lasted almost half a day, we passed through several gates in the succession of inner defensive walls. Each was already open to receive us, but I noted that they closed behind us after we had passed through, cutting off any possibility of retreat.

Eyes watched us from narrow windows far above, but I knew that no friends gazed down upon me. We haizda mages lived and worked far from the dissident groups and shifting alliances of the city's inhabitants.

At last we reached the main gate, and here the walls towered up, lost to sight amongst the clouds. Covered in ice and snow, Valkarky appeared more like the vertical face of a mountain peak; the open gates were like the entrance to some wonderful dark cavern, full of unknown delights.

Two mounted Shaiksa assassins, lances at the ready, waited on either side of these huge gates, but they had rivals who would compete to seize me: three score of foot militia had lined up, their captain holding my arrest warrant with his left hand extended over his head in the traditional manner. The red seal formed from the spit and coagulated blood of the Triumvirate was clearly visible.

The Rowler girls gasped in shock at the sight that greeted us. But of course, none of my enemies could touch me if I could persuade the Triumvirate to allow me legal entry.

I believed it could be done, but I must first deal with their instrument, the gatekeeper known as the Kashilowa, which now undulated its way towards us, its long, pulsing body bristling with spines and its breath billowing into the cold air in great clouds. At first it was hidden by the cloud of snow kicked up by its thousand legs, but this slowly settled and it was fully revealed to us. The single Kashilowa and the myriad whoskor had been created in order to serve the needs of the city. It was all part of the magic of the High Mages.

Immediately, clearly terrified, the smallest sister began to scream at the top of her lungs, and Nessa brought her horse alongside my own, trying to comfort her. But before she could do so, Susan fainted away, and it took all

Nessa's strength to prevent her from falling from their horse.

Even brave Nessa moaned in terror when the gatekeeper scuttled forward and touched her forehead with the tip of the long tongue that spiralled from its mouth. It was simply tasting her skin to determine her fitness to enter Valkarky, so I don't know why she found it so alarming. All purrai in transit are subject to the most stringent health checks to make sure that no contagion is brought into the city.

Our two horses were Kobalos-trained, but the proximity of the gatekeeper caused their nostrils to flare and their eyes to dilate; they trembled with fear. This was hardly surprising: when the huge creature yawned to feign boredom, opening its jaws to their full extent, its mouth was so big it could have swallowed them whole.

'Speak!' the Kashilowa commanded, directing its one hundred eyes in my direction. Its voice was as loud as a thunderclap, and that one word brought down dozens of long icicles from the overhang of the wall above the gate. One of the spears of ice impaled a militiaman, whose blood began to stain the snow an appealing shade of red – almost as lovely as the lambskin rugs in my old ghanbala tree. One glance made my mouth start to water and I found it difficult to concentrate on the business in hand.

Fortunately the Kashilowa's movement had disturbed the multitude of winged parasites that sheltered amongst its prickly spines. Quickly I reached out and plucked a few from the air, before they could settle again, and stuffed them into my mouth. Their own blood combined with that of

their host was a tasty blend and assuaged a little of my
hunger.

Now, I gathered my thoughts and, not wishing to appear
intimidated, leaped from my horse and grew to my largest
size so that my eyes were level with the gatekeeper's teeth. I
amplified my voice too, dislodging another shower of icicles.
This time no one was harmed; the militia had sensibly with-
drawn to a safe distance.

All those present at the gates knew my identity and what my
business was. Nevertheless it was necessary to make a formal
statement.

'I demand entry to Valkarky!' I cried. 'I have been wronged
by a High Mage and a band of his accomplices, including a
Shaiksa assassin, who conspired together to illegally appropriate my three purrai for their own use. I request a hearing
before the Triumvirate!'

'Where is this High Mage whom you claim appropriated
your property? Who are these three purrai who accompany
you? Are they the same ones you refer to? If so, they are now in
your possession, so how has a crime been committed?' asked
the Kashilowa.

'Yes, they are the same. I seized them back, as was my right,
using only minimal force. Unfortunately, in defending myself, I
was forced to slay the High Mage and the Shaiksa assassin.
Additionally, a hyb warrior waylaid me on the road to Valkarky
and I was forced to kill him too. It is all very regrettable but
necessary.'

'Your story is questionable. How could a haizda mage such

as yourself confront and slay a Shaiksa assassin, a High Mage and a hyb? What is your name?'

It already knew my name, but this was a formality of question and answer that I could not avoid; the ritual necessary to gain entry to the city.

'My name is Slither and I did just what was necessary. Perhaps the red eye of the Dog Star looked down on me favourably, thus accounting for my victory.'

'*Slither?* What kind of a name is that?'

The Kashilowa was no longer giving me the respect I felt was my due. I would not allow it to deride me. So I answered it with venom in my voice. It was no more than it deserved.

'It is the name I chose for myself when I came of age in the early spring of my seventieth year. It is the sound I make when I swing with my tail from a high branch of my ghanbala tree. It is the sound I make when I become very small and creep through a gap in a wall or floor to gain access to a locked, secret or private place. It is also the sound and sensation that an enemy is aware of when I creep into his brain. Allow me to demonstrate!'

Feeling insulted that the gatekeeper should bring the suitability of my chosen name into question, I spat into the nearest of its hundred eyes. I had quickly combined with my saliva two substances that cause instant itchiness and irritation. Simultaneously my mind slithered into its brain.

The reaction of the gatekeeper was somewhat extreme. It must have had a low toleration of pain. It leaped backwards so quickly that most of its thousand legs became entangled; it lost its balance and rolled sideways in the snow, crushing another unfortunate militiaman.

Do you like the sensation of slither? I asked, speaking my words straight into its head.

Enough! Enough! it cried – although of all the sentient minds around, I was the only one who heard it, its thoughts trembling within my head.

Allow me my rights! I demanded. *Grant me entry into Valkarky and a hearing before the Triumvirate and I will ease the discomfort in your eyes and slither right out of your brain.*

Yes! Yes! I grant it! it said.

Keeping my promise, I withdrew from its head. It rolled back onto most of its feet and brought its head close so that my horse began to tremble even more violently and little Nessa began to moan with terror. Quickly I spat into its nearest eye for a second time. This time my saliva contained an antidote to the irritation.

However, it was a long time before it spoke, and for a moment I feared betrayal. 'I must test you to verify your claims,' it growled.

I nodded acceptance, and now it was my turn to feel the touch of its long tongue on my forehead. It would be able to taste whether I was lying or not. At last the tongue withdrew back into its cavernous mouth.

'You *believe* that you are telling the truth. But lies can sometimes be cloaked by magic. Nevertheless, your claims deserve further investigation. Would you submit to a rigorous probing?' it asked.

'Willingly,' I said.

'On that condition, I grant entry to the city and a hearing for this haizda mage!' it cried out, and it was done.

I leaned down and whispered into Nessa's ear, 'That wasn't too bad, was it? I promised your father that I would look after you, and I am certainly keeping that promise!'

Thus we were given permission to enter Valkarky, and our enemies could do nothing to prevent it. The two younger sisters were hysterical now, while even brave Nessa was clearly struggling with the prospect of entering our beautiful city. So I breathed into each of their faces in turn, using boska, and caused them to fall into a very deep sleep.

So long as I lived, they were safe. So long as I kept them in separate rooms in my own quarters and always accompanied them in public in the appropriate manner, the law would protect them.

I walked through the gates, my head held high, while the sisters were carried inside by the Kobalos servants summoned by the gatekeeper. We haizda mages rarely visit Valkarky, but in case it ever proves necessary, we maintain quarters here, along with a small number of servants to receive us. Within an hour I was safe in that refuge, all my needs attended to while the sisters slept.

What lucky girls they were to have such a benevolent owner!

First I tried to wake Nessa.

I had already breathed into her face to counter the effects of boska, but her eyes remained stubbornly shut. She was proving very difficult to rouse, and for a few moments I feared that in my haste to render her unconscious, I had made the chemical mixture too strong and damaged her brain. This happens only rarely, but it is always a risk. My error would have been forgivable. After all, I had been occupied with my negotiations with the gatekeeper and had other, more important things on my mind.

I studied her face, willing her to wake up. My anxiety growing, I began to call out her name.

CHAPTER 13
THE HAGGENBROOD

❧NESSA❧

'Wake up, little Nessa!' cried a voice. It seemed to come from a great distance. I was in a deep, comfortable sleep and just wanted to be left alone. Then I was shaken roughly by the shoulder.

The moment I opened my eyes I was filled with the extreme terror that comes to one whose nightmare follows her back to the waking world. Instantly I remembered the horrors before the gates of Valkarky and the terrible sensation of choking when Slither breathed into my face. I had fallen into darkness, believing that I was dying. But it wasn't that which caused my heart to flutter and my whole body to shake. Nor was it the snarl on the face of the beast as he shook me.

What made me shrink away to the far corner of my bed was the thing that I saw behind him.

'There is no need to be afraid,' Slither told me in his gruff voice. 'For the present you are quite safe. This is the refuge for haizda mages visiting Valkarky.'

I took several shallow breaths and managed to point over his right shoulder at the horrific thing on the wall. He looked back at it and then gave the travesty of a smile.

It looked like an extremely large human head with six thin, multi-jointed legs sprouting from the place where its ears should have been. It had long hair but neither eyes nor a nose. There wasn't room for them. A huge oval mouth took up most of its face, and from it protruded three long thick tongues covered with backward-facing barbs. It seemed to be licking the walls, making a harsh rhythmical rasping sound as it did so.

'Because these quarters are rarely used, they are subject to fungal growth. What you see is just a harmless *sklutch*, one of the lesser servants that we employ. It is merely going about its routine duties, cleaning the walls with its tongues and sucking up the loose fragments. There is no need to be afraid, little Nessa. It is simply a diligent servant, but as it disturbs you I will send it away immediately.'

With those words he clapped his hands very hard. The hideous creature stopped its cleaning at once and raised two front antennae which, until then, had been hidden by

115

its long hair. They twitched and revolved in a slow circle.

Slither gave three more claps, and it immediately scuttled down the wall and retired to a narrow crevice near the floor.

'The sklutch, with its soft brown hair, thin black legs and efficient tongues, is perfectly formed and suited to its task, little Nessa. It never ceases to astonish me how such a plump creature is able, without the use of magic, to fold itself into such a narrow crack. Anyway, how are you feeling now?'

Suddenly I felt ashamed. My own fears had dominated everything and I had forgotten all about Bryony and Susan. 'Where are my sisters?' I demanded, rising up onto my knees.

'They are quite safe, but according to Kobalos custom each purra must be housed in a separate room. I can behave no differently here than I did in the kulad. Besides, your sisters are still sleeping.'

'They weren't safe in that tower. Why should this be any different?'

'Fear not, Nessa. This is Valkarky, a city ruled by law where everyone watches. That kulad was under the control of a corrupt High Mage with no respect for the property of others. I assure you that it will be different here.'

I shook my head in disbelief. 'How long have I been asleep?' I asked.

'A few hours at the most. While you slept, I was given a hearing and subjected to a deep probing which was quite painful. However, it was worth it – they reached a decision quickly.'

I felt a surge of hope. 'So we can leave this place now?'

'I wish it were that simple, little Nessa. It was proven that I was telling the truth, and the Triumvirate were prepared to absolve me of all guilt in law, but the Shaiksa Brotherhood made a formal objection; they submitted false evidence that was impossible to refute. They communicated the dying thoughts of the assassin that I slew. He accused me of theft, saying that Nunc, the High Mage, had paid me well for ownership of you and your two plump sisters.

'I do not accuse the dead assassin of having lied. It may well be that he only repeated information that had been given him by Nunc. However, he lives no more, so now it is his dead, deceitful word against my honest living one.' Slither paused a moment and I held my breath in anticipation of what he would say next.

'I must face trial by combat. There are many legal disputes each year – a counter claim over ownership of purrai is just one of the categories of civil conflict. The vast majority are resolved directly by the Triumvirate, but in difficult cases the accused must face such a trial. It is outrageous that I have been placed in such a position – I need to vent my anger. Now I have been given the opportunity to do so publicly.'

'You have to fight? Against another of the mages?' Fear clutched my heart again. If he lost, what would happen to us?

'No, little Nessa. I only wish that were so. I must face the *Haggenbrood*.'

I didn't even like the sound of the word. 'What is that?' I asked. 'Some kind of creature like the ones who are building the walls of this city?' They were indeed hideous things.

'In a way, yes, but the Haggenbrood was created by the magic of the High Mages to fight in ritual combat; that is its sole purpose in life. It consists of three warrior entities bred from the flesh of a purra. The three share a common mind, and are, to all intents and purposes, one creature.'

'Can you defeat it?'

'No one has ever done so before.'

'That's not fair! If you are certain to lose, how can it be a "trial by combat"?'

'It is the way of things. It allows a modicum of hope, and is more honourable than being executed. And, of course, victory is not impossible – there is always a first time for everything. We cannot afford to be pessimistic, little Nessa.'

'If you die, will we be slaves or will they kill us as well?' I managed to ask – though I didn't really want to hear the answer. 'Could you not keep your promise to my father and send my two sisters to safety before your trial?'

'I only wish I could. But who would be willing to escort you out of the city? It is impossible. Without me you have no status here other than as slaves or food. If I die, then you will die there in the arena with me, slain by the claws and teeth of the Haggenbrood. I must defend you against the creature or die in the attempt. Come, I will show you so that you can prepare your mind for what lies ahead.'

I was so frustrated by the situation we were in. Even though Slither repulsed me, I was dependent on him for survival. The beast left the room for a few moments, leaving me alone with my sombre thoughts, but returned clutching a long chain and a lock.

'Come here!' he commanded. 'I must place this around your neck.'

'Why?' I asked. 'I won't try to run away. Where could I go? As you pointed out, without your protection I would be killed on sight!'

'Within Valkarky, a purra may only appear in public in the presence of her owner, with this chain around her neck. Without the chain you would indeed be taken and there would be nothing I could do about it. This is the law.'

I scowled at the beast, but knew I had no choice but to submit. He carefully placed the cold metal chain about my neck and then attached a small lock to complete and maintain the circle. Then, holding the rest of the chain in his left hand, he gave a small tug as if I were an animal, and pointed towards the door.

'Now, purra, I will lead you to the arena!' he declared.

He led me along a seemingly endless succession of gloomy corridors. Mostly they were lit by flickering torches, but in some sections the walls themselves seemed to radiate a white light. Kobalos that we passed mostly ignored us, gazing straight ahead. But when the rare curious glance came our way, Slither invariably gave a tug on the chain, jerking my head forward sharply. On one such occasion an involuntary cry escaped my lips and tears came into my eyes. But when we were once again alone in the corridor, the beast turned and spoke to me in hushed tones.

'I have been gentle, little Nessa, and the chain is not tight. Some owners fix them so tightly that the purra is always red in the face and struggling for breath. Be brave. You will need all your courage in the arena!'

He turned, tugged the chain again and we continued on our way. The city was vast, but so gloomy that it seemed as if we were underground. Even the open spaces accessed by the corridors looked like vast caverns, but their walls were perfectly smooth and clearly manufactured rather than being of natural stone.

At one point we passed through what appeared to be a vast food market. Kobalos were handing over coins and receiving metal basins in return. Some seemed to contain roots or fungi, but in others small worm-like creatures squirmed as the purchasers greedily stuffed them into their mouths. I could barely contain the bile rising from my stomach at the sight and the smell.

Then there were larger vats. Looking more closely, I saw with horror that they were full of blood, from which steam was rising. Each was surrounded by a throng of jostling Kobalos dipping in metal cups and quaffing the liquid greedily, so that it dribbled down their chins and splattered on the floor.

What manner of creatures had died to fill those vats? Valkarky was a terrible, terrifying, ugly place. And were it ever to expand to cover the whole world, as Slither had boasted, it would create a hell on earth – every bit of grass, every tree, every flower and creature of the meadows replaced by this vast monstrosity.

It was not only Kobalos that I glimpsed. There were other creatures that made me shudder with fear, and even in the presence of Slither I did not feel safe. Mostly they resembled insects, except that the smallest creature I saw was the size of a sheepdog, while the largest could have bitten off my head with ease. I hoped my sisters were still safely asleep in their rooms.

Some creatures scuttled overhead on many legs, as if they were messengers on urgent business, while others loitered, perhaps performing a similar cleaning function to the servant in Slither's quarters.

But one thing puzzled me. I saw Kobalos and I saw chained human female slaves, but why did I not see any Kobalos females? Were they not allowed out in public? The faces of the Kobalos were all hairy and bestial, with elongated jaws and sharp teeth. Could it be that Kobalos females were similar to the males in appearance and I simply couldn't tell the difference?

We twisted and turned through this labyrinth until we arrived at a wide flight of gleaming white steps. Four levels up, we finally reached a huge gate large enough to admit a creature ten times my size.

'Here we are, little Nessa. This is where we will all die or triumph!' Slither said, pulling me through.

I found myself standing on a triangular platform surrounded by tiers of empty seats rising on either side to encircle us completely.

'The whole arena is formed from *skoya*. The whoskor spat it into a mound so that it could be manipulated and shaped by their many nine-fingered hands.'

'It's so white!' I exclaimed. It dazzled my eyes.

'Skoya can be many colours,' Slither explained, 'but there is a reason why it is white, little Nessa. It makes it easier to see the bright red of freshly spilled blood, a colour that is very exciting to my people.'

This place was truly despicable. I did not reply, but my eyes moved around, darting in all directions as I wondered about the layout of the arena. I saw that there was a white post positioned at each corner of the triangular arena.

'What are those for?' I asked.

'They are the three posts to which you and your two sisters will be tethered. The number varies, and the arena is shaped anew in preparation for each trial. But it is always white, to display the blood of the defeated to its best effect. You will be bound there, and the Haggenbrood will try to drink your blood then eat you. I will do my best to save you all.'

My stomach churned at the impossibility of the task. What was this Haggenbrood? I was certain my sisters and I would all die here.

'Do you see that?' Slither asked, pointing to the circular grille in the floor at the centre of the triangular arena.

I was filled with a terrible foreboding and I began to tremble. I did not even want to look at the grille, let alone move closer to it. But I had no choice.

He started to walk towards it, tugging me after him. All at once I smelled something foul, and was afraid to move closer.

When I came to a halt, the chain jerked my neck painfully. Rather than tug me forward again, Slither walked back to see what my problem was.

'What ails you, little Nessa?'

'That awful stench! What is it? Is it from something down there?' I pointed with a trembling finger towards the grille.

Slither tilted his head and sniffed the air. 'Yes. What you smell is the scent of the Haggenbrood. That it where it will emerge. Come closer and take a look,' he said, walking towards the centre of the arena.

Once again the chain became taut as I resisted. But this time Slither gave a hard tug and I reluctantly stumbled along after him until we approached the edge of the pit.

'Look down through the grille, little Nessa, and tell me what you see.'

The grille was wide-meshed and white, but the inside of the pit was a dark brown. It was coated with something extremely unpleasant. Up close, the stink was unbearable, and I tried to pull away.

'The Haggenbrood excretes that brown slime from its three bodies as part of its digestive process. It is that which causes the stench. Don't be afraid. Move closer so you can see properly.'

Cautiously I moved to edge of the pit and looked down into the darkness. I felt very nervous and vulnerable, and my legs trembled. Why did Slither want me to stand so close? The grille looked too flimsy to bear my weight. His hand touched my shoulder, and for one terrifying moment I thought he was about to push me in.

'There's something moving down there!' I cried, shaking with fear. Down below, in spite of the darkness, I could see three pairs of glowing red eyes watching me!

The next moment, something leaped upwards, and the long, scaly fingers of a huge hand grasped the grille. The creature roared up at us through the bars, clearly desperate to sink its teeth into my flesh. I had a glimpse of its snarling mouth, angry red eyes and pointed ears.

This was what we faced. My knees began to tremble more violently and my heart pounded with fear. What chance did Slither have against three such fearsome beasts? We were as good as dead.

But my captor showed no fear, and with a frown moved on to the grille directly above the snarling face of the creature. 'Learn your place! I walk the earth and you belong in the filth!' he shouted into its teeth, stamping down hard on its fingers with his boots. With an angry growl, the Haggenbrood released its hold and fell back into the pit.

'Never show fear to such creatures, little Nessa,' he advised me. 'Always be bold! It pays to show them exactly whom they will be dealing with in the arena.'

'It's so fast and fierce.' I shook my head in dismay. 'What hope do you have against three of them? You will be alone. Surely you should have some help?'

'Oh, Nessa, you must try to listen more carefully to what I say. It is even worse than that. As I explained, the

Haggenbrood is *one* creature. One mind controls the three bodies, three *selves*, and can coordinate their attack as easily as I can control each of my fingers simultaneously.'

In order to demonstrate, he lowered his hairy hand and drummed a quick rhythm on the side of my head with three of his fingers. It hurt and I gave a cry of pain. Next he quickly flexed those same fingers, making his knucklebones crack repeatedly. I shivered.

'You will be immobile, tied to the posts, and I will only be able to be in one place at a time. Although I will try, it may prove impossible to defend all three of you. I will be alone, of course, because those are the rules. Only my purrai and I are allowed in the arena to face the Haggenbrood.'

'Then don't worry about me,' I told him. 'Defend my sisters.'

I had spoken without thinking, but I would not recant. Although I was desperately afraid of the Haggenbrood, I couldn't bear the thought of what they might do to Bryony and Susan.

'That is very noble of you, little one, but that depends on how the Haggenbrood deploys its selves.'

'Can't you take the initiative and attack first?' I asked.

'Must I explain it again? There are rules, little Nessa, and I am bound by them. They vary from trial to trial, adjusted to take account of the number of purrai involved. But this is the situation here and we must abide by it. Firstly the grille will be removed and the Haggenbrood will climb out of the pit. Once its three selves are in position, the signal will be given to begin. I can only react to the attack, which could be aimed at any one of you. Alternatively, it may ignore you and launch an all-out assault on me. That way, once I am dead, the Haggenbrood can feed from you and your plump sisters at its leisure. Also, if it attacks you first and two of you die, I must surrender my weapons and let it kill me. Those are the rules of this trial.'

I couldn't believe I was discussing something so brutal. 'What weapons are you permitted?'

'As many blades as I wish.'

'Then cut me free and give me a blade. If I move, it might distract it and give you a better chance. We must get my sisters to safety.'

Again the words had flown from my lips without prior thought. But reflecting quickly, I perceived that they were wise indeed. It might just give my sisters a chance of life, and surely it was better to die with a knife in my hand than bound helpless to a post?

I saw the astonishment on the beast's face. He frowned and seemed to be considering the possibility.

'Would that be allowed?' I persisted, breaking the silence that had come between us.

'There is nothing in the rules that forbids me to cut you free,' he admitted. 'Your offer is generous indeed. But while the Haggenbrood is prevented by its conditioning not to leave the arena, you could do so. And therein lies the danger. If you did so, the trial would immediately be over and all our lives would be forfeit. How brave are you, little Nessa? Could you stand your ground when teeth and claws snap in your face?'

'Yes,' I replied immediately. 'It might give us a chance.'

But could I? Would I really be brave enough to distract this terrible, fearsome Haggenbrood?

'Even if you are not torn to pieces, the Haggenbrood has glands which secrete a deadly poison. If even the tip of one claw pierces your skin it results in *kirrhos*, which we call the 'tawny death'. It is ugly to look upon and worse to suffer. There is no cure. So can you *make* your little human body obey your will, little Nessa? Terror may cause it to disobey you. Once you flee the arena, we are all dead. One small step would be enough!'

I took a deep breath. Yes, I would do it. Despite my dislike of Slither, the situation had made us allies and I would have to work alongside him to give my sisters some hope of survival.

'I am sure that I won't run. I want to give my sisters a chance of life.'

Slither stared at me hard. 'To release a captive during trial by combat is unprecedented,' he said. 'It would be a complete surprise to everybody, including the Haggenbrood.'

Then, without another word, he tugged at the chain and led me back through Valkarky to his quarters.

CHAPTER 14
GOSSIP AND NEWS

Using a whetstone, I systematically began to sharpen the blades I planned to use in the arena. I selected two daggers – along with Old Rowler's sabre, which had quickly become my favourite weapon.

As I worked, Nessa watched me intently. I was considering her surprise proposal. She was, without doubt, brave – far braver than any other purra I had encountered, but there was a terrible risk in letting her stand in the arena unbound. If she fled, I would forfeit my life. I sensed that she was about to say something important to her, and was soon proved correct.

'I would like to ask you a favour,' she said at last.

'Speak and I will listen,' I replied, concentrating most of my attention on the task at hand but prepared to give her a hearing.

'Could my sisters be bound to their posts without being awoken?' she asked. 'I would like to spare them the terror of the arena.'

'That is impossible, little Nessa. It would not be allowed – it would deprive those who witness the trial of the pleasure of hearing them scream. And it is more enjoyable to watch some-one who is conscious bleed and die. Asleep, they would provide no entertainment at all.'

As a youngster, I had once visited a trial. It had been over very quickly, but despite that I had enjoyed the manner in which the Haggenbrood despatched its victims, and the way the blood splattered, making delightful patterns against the white of the arena floor. But on my rare visits to Valkarky since taking up my vocation, I had never even considered attending another.

Now I was comfortable alone, working my haizda, and preferred to be far from the clamour of such events. I no longer found it comfortable to be close to so many of my people in one place.

'Entertainment?! How can you use such a word when my sisters' young lives might be lost? What kind of creatures are you?'

'It is just the way things are, little Nessa. We are very different to humans. It is the way of my people, and I am bound by Kobalos customs and conventions. So I can do nothing to spare you and your delicious sisters the inevitable fear and pain that awaits you.'

It never ceased to amaze me that Nessa was prepared to sacrifice herself to help her sisters. Of course, for her to stand and face even one of the Haggenbrood's selves in such a way, even with a knife in her puny hand, could have only one result. She would be dead before she realized what had happened. But I thought such bravery deserved a reward.

What would she most wish for now? I wondered. In a second I had the answer. Briefly I would suspend the solitary confinement of the three purrai.

'Would you like me to wake your sisters now so that you can have a little time alone? It might be your last chance to talk together?' I offered – very generously, I thought.

'Yes, please, I would like that,' Nessa said solemnly. 'How long is it before the trial?'

'Almost a full day, so enjoy yourselves and make the best of the time that remains. I will bring your two plump sisters here, then leave you alone to talk in privacy for a while.'

So, keeping my promise, I brought the three sisters together. Of course, I did not give them privacy because I was very curious to hear what they had to say to each other, so I made myself very small and slithered into the room using a drainage hole in the floor as my means of access.

'I wish I had clean clothes and a blue ribbon for my hair,' Susan said plaintively.

'I'm sure you'll have all you need once you're safe in

Pwodente,' Nessa replied. 'Whatever happens we are going to survive. You've got to believe that.'

'I'm sorry,' Susan said, shaking her head as tears sprang to her eyes. 'I'll try, but I'm not as brave as you, Nessa. I'll try to do better. I really will.'

It didn't seem worth staying any longer – the sisters had little of interest to say to each other. Nessa tried to remain calm but, after Susan had complimented her on being brave, every time she started to speak, her bottom lip began to tremble as if it had a life of its own. When she finally did manage to utter a few sentences, all three sisters burst into tears and spent the rest of the time that remained to them sobbing and hugging each other tightly. It was all very futile.

I was sorry to be facing death. Now I would never attain my full potential. I needed at least a further century of study before I could complete my mastery of haizda magic and hone my fighting skills to their optimum level. It would also have been pleasing to learn that I had overcome the dangerous threat of skaiium, avoiding the weakness that afflicts some of our order. Now I would never know the outcome. However, I decided to make the best of what might well be the last day of my life in this world, so I went to my private room and snapped my fingers five times to summon Hom, a type of homunculus, who is perhaps the most interesting servant deployed in Valkarky by haizda mages. He is a gatherer of news and gossip, and his multiple shapes are specially formed for that task.

One, which is in the form of a rat, functions particularly well in the sewers, making it possible for his specially adapted ears to listen in to conversations all over the city; while submerged he can focus his hearing on a conversation despite many intervening skoya floors and walls.

Another of his selves has powerful wings and can soar far above the city to view its rooftops and thus see anyone approaching or leaving Valkarky.

The self that gives its reports takes the form of a very small figure not unlike a human male. Of course, it is covered with long brown fur in order to keep it warm, and always lives within our haizda quarters while its other industrious bodies roam far and wide. Once it had squeezed out of its hole, it clambered up onto the chair directly opposite my own.

'Report on the progress of all other haizda mages!' I commanded.

Never in the course of my visits to Valkarky had I found another haizda mage in residence here. Indeed, it was many years since I had encountered the last one while journeying along the edge of the human territories far to the southeast. We had spent a few hours together and exchanged little more than pleasantries – we were by nature secretive. But each haizda mage made a report to Hom before leaving the city, and that information was available to me now.

'In addition to yourself, eleven others have visited and reported in the last thirty years,' Hom said. 'No doubt you will be interested to know that eighteen months ago Rasptail made what he believed might be his final visit here. He is now almost eight hundred years old and fears that his powers are beginning their slow decline. Once he becomes certain of it, he proposes to end his life.'

Hom was correct in his assumption that I would be interested in news of Rasptail. After all, he was the haizda who had trained me during my noviciate, the thirty-year period that begins the vocation. After that a haizda mage must study and develop alone. Rasptail had been a harsh but fair master, and I was saddened to hear that his powers were waning. It was the haizda way to take one's life at that point. We chose death rather than a long decline.

Next he gave report of the last known status of the other ten mages. By the time he finished I was weary of it and demanded information about Valkarky and its inhabitants.

'What would you like first, master – news or gossip?' Hom asked in his thin reedy voice.

News is usually quite predictable – variations on events that have been repeated in our city over many centuries. For example, there is the rate at which Valkarky is expanding; some years growth is slower, and that always gives cause for concern to those who worry about such things. Then there are statistics on the execution of prisoners – usually criminals. I find most of that quite boring.

However, I like gossip; it occasionally has some foundation in fact.

'Give me the most interesting gossip,' I instructed, noting that Hom was looking rather bedraggled, his fur matted and tinged with grey. He was getting old, and would soon have to be replaced.

'The thing most talked about, master, is that a large star-stone has fallen to earth not too far from the city. As it heated up, passing through the air, it took on the most interesting crimson hue, suggesting that it is composed of ore perfect for constructing blades. Many are out searching for it.'

Star-stone was very valuable, but it was likely that seeking it was a fools' errand. It had probably burned up before impact – or maybe they had been mistaken about the colour. Such objects, with their spectacular pyrotechnic displays, were frequently seen but rarely found. It might even have been the same one I glimpsed to the north. But, if so, I had seen no hint of crimson.

'Anything else?' I demanded.

'It is rumoured that a lone purra was in the area where the stone fell. She was taken prisoner, but at great cost to the Oussa. They say that she resisted and that at least four of them died.'

Now, this was very interesting, but most improbable. The Oussa were the guard who answered directly to the Triumvirate, which was composed of the three most powerful High Mages in the city. For one person to kill four of their elite guard was even more unlikely than my own feat of slaying a Shaiksa assassin. And, after all, I am a haizda mage, not a lone female.

Suddenly I felt a great surge of curiosity. 'I would like to see her corpse,' I said. 'Do they talk of where it is to be found?'

'They say that she was taken alive and is being held within one of the most secure of the Oussa dungeons.'

'Taken alive?!' I exclaimed. That was even more unlikely.

'Investigate this further,' I commanded. 'Report back as soon as you are able. I want to know where the purra is being held.'

Hom scuttled back to his hole, while I busied myself making preparations for my battle against the Haggenbrood. I began with mental exercises in which I visualized the steps leading up to victory. Firstly I placed myself in the arena; next, in my mind's eye, I watched the Haggenbrood haul its three ugly selves out of the pit. I concentrated until I could both see and smell the creature. Gradually I regulated my breathing, making the image sharper, but I had only completed the preliminary sequence, entering the first level of concentration, when Hom reappeared and took his place once more on the chair opposite me.

'Speak!' I commanded. 'What have you learned?'

'I can now upgrade both reports from "gossip" to "news". The star-stone was found by the Oussa and brought back to the city with the purra. The present location of the stone is unknown, but the purra is being held in District Yaksa Central, Level Thirteen, cell forty-two.'

That was the most secure dungeon complex in the city, and cell forty-two was usually reserved for only the most dangerous and resourceful of prisoners. How could a mere purra be deserving of such an honour?

I felt an immediate compulsion to see her for myself. I had far more time than I needed to complete my preparations for battle, so this would prove an interesting distraction. Quickly dismissing Hom, I set out for District Yaksa Central without delay.

Being honour-bound to attend the trial by combat, my movements through the city were not restricted. However, once I reached the security zone I was likely to be questioned and even arrested if I disregarded warnings about proceeding further.

So I made myself as small as possible, and then used magic strong enough to cloak myself against all but the most powerful of observers. Only the very strongest mages and assassins would now be able to see me. The security guards could no doubt penetrate the normal cloaking devices of city mages, but I was a haizda, and luckily our methods were largely unknown.

Level by level I began to descend. At first the corridors and concourses were thronged with Kobalos. I strolled through the lavish multicoloured malls where rich merchants displayed their goods for even richer customers, while others could only gape and dream. This gave way three levels lower to the food stalls where hawkers cooked blood, bone and offal over open fires, filling the air with pungent odours.

My favourite place here was the blood vats where, for the price of two valcrons, you could drink as much as you wanted. I extended my tongue until I could lap the thickest most viscous part of the delightful liquid and then, my belly full to bursting, continued my descent.

After a while I left the Kobalos crowds far behind, encountering only the occasional guard; cloaked as I was, I was able to slip past them with ease. By the time I reached Level Twelve, the only things that moved were the whoskor or other similar entities. At one point I glimpsed a huge worm-like creature that regarded me from the mouth of a dark tunnel, its single gigantic bleary eye following my progress. I had no name for it. It was new to me, no doubt spawned as the result of some new magic developed by the High Mages. What disturbed me momentarily was that it could see me despite my cloaking. But it slid slowly back into the tunnel and showed no further interest in my progress downwards.

It took me almost an hour to penetrate to Level Thirteen. Less than five minutes later I was standing outside cell forty-two. Torches flickered on the walls of the dank corridor, which were not constructed from skoya – these dungeons had been carved out of the bed-rock far below the city. I heard groans all around, and the occasional scream cut through the air, making my mouth fill with saliva. Then someone began to beg:

'No! No!' the voice cried out plaintively. 'Hurt me no more! It is too much! I confess! I confess! I did all that you accuse me of. But please stop. I wish to—'

The voice became a scream of agony, which meant that the torture had continued and no doubt intensified. I enjoyed that, but I must tell you that I could never be a torturer of the weak. I much prefer to inflict pain in battle, testing myself against another who shows courage and mettle.

These delightful sounds came from cells where enemies of Valkarky were being confined. They were being tortured, and deservedly so. It was a pleasure to hear their cries of pain. But from cell forty-two there came no sound. Was the purra dead? No doubt she had been too weak to withstand the clever tortures applied.

I slithered under the door to find that things were quite different from what I had expected. Instantly I knew that the prisoner was very much alive. Not only that – despite my cloaking magic, she could see me. She stared down at me in a way that left me in no doubt about it. It was also clear that she considered me to be no better than an insect that she would crush under her heel.

Of course, she was in no position to do that because she was nailed to the wall with silver-alloy pins. There was one through each wrist and each foot. In addition, a silver chain was twisted around her neck, pulled taut and fastened to a large hook in the ceiling of the dungeon. That was not to mention the fact that her lips were stitched together with silver twine so she could not speak. I sensed that she was in considerable pain, and it was a wonder that she was not moaning.

She was not dressed in a skirt – the usual garb of both city purrai and those from outside. Her garment was divided and strapped tightly to each thigh. On her upper body was a short brown smock tied at the waist.

I blew myself up to a height that brought us face to face and decided that I needed to speak with this purra. No doubt they had sewn her lips shut for a purpose, and some risk might be involved in removing the stitches, but I was curious to know more. I drew a blade, and with its sharp tip very carefully sliced through the silver twine. Then I tugged it free with a jerk so that her swollen lips fell open.

What I saw within her mouth surprised me. Her teeth had been filed to points.

'Who are you?' I demanded.

She smiled at me then. It was not the smile of a bound prisoner. It was an expression that might have flickered onto her face had our roles been reversed.

'I've been waiting for you to visit me,' she said, ignoring my question. 'Why has it taken you so long?'

'Waiting for me?' I asked. 'How can that be?'

Her expression became stern and imperious – totally inappropriate for a purra. 'I summoned you to my presence two hours ago, little mage,' she said.

What madness was this? For a moment I was lost for words.

Then she smiled very widely to display all her pointy teeth.

'I am Grimalkin,' she said.

CHAPTER 15
GRIMALKIN

I regarded her with astonishment.

'You speak your name as if I should know it. I have never heard of a purra called Grimalkin. You claim you "summoned" me? What foolish talk is that?' I demanded.

'It is the truth,' she said. 'Once I had discovered everything there was to know about you, I summoned you by magic using a spell of compulsion. There is the instrument of your undoing!'

With a slight flick of her eyebrows, she indicated the far corner of her cell. One of Hom's rat-bodied selves was lying there. Its eyes were closed and its thin tail was twitching as if it was in the grip of some seizure.

'Even with my lips bound, it was easy to gain control of such a foolish creature. When it came looking for me, I sucked from its busybody self all the knowledge I needed. It was then very easy to bring you here. I know all about you, mage. I know the trouble that you are in. And I am prepared to help you, but I will need three things in return.'

'Help me? You are in no position to help anyone! And soon you will be dead. Four members of the Oussa lost their lives attempting to bring you into lawful custody. Your death warrant will already have been signed. No doubt they will delay your demise in order to prolong your pain and learn what they can about you.'

'There was nothing lawful about my capture,' the purra retorted. 'They stole from me a piece of star ore that was in my possession. Other more important things were also confiscated. These you must return to me in order to receive my help.'

So the purra *had* found the star-stone. 'Finders keepers' was the law in such cases, but the Oussa would not accept that a lone human, especially a purra who was so close to Valkarky, had any rights. A star-stone was rare, very valuable and much sought after. A weapon using such ore could be fashioned only by the most skilled of smiths, but properly worked the result was a blade that never lost its edge and could not be broken. Even if the star-stone had not been a factor, this purra would have been arrested on sight and either eaten or bound in slavery. That she had resisted meant certain death.

By rights I should have left her to her fate, but I was filled with an overwhelming curiosity and wanted to learn more. I

was also impressed by her bravery and combat ability in slaying four of the Oussa.

'If you were free, how could you help me?' I asked.

'You face trial by combat against a creature that you call the
Haggenbrood. It has never been defeated, so history says that
you will lose and die . . .'

I raised my hand to protest but she continued speaking, a
little more rapidly than before.

'Don't try to deny it. I know all about you – information from
the mind of your little spy. I know the situation and have
thought out what to do. I could take the place of one of the
three girls bound to stakes in the arena – the one called Nessa
is the closest to me in size; I hold her image in my mind,
courtesy of your spy. Cut me free and give me a blade as you
intended for her. I will fight alongside you; consequently, the
Haggenbrood will die and you will be allowed to leave the city
with the three girls.'

'This is foolish,' I told her, aghast at the way she had
entered my head. 'I don't know why I am wasting my time
listening to you. Even if I could free you from this cell, do you
not think that your substitution for little Nessa would be
noticed?'

The purra smiled and her whole body seemed to shimmer,
and then I had a moment of dizziness. And there before me, the
silver pins through her hands and feet, the silver chain twisted
tightly about her neck, was Nessa.

'Now do you believe?' she asked, speaking with the voice of
little Nessa, the intonation and nuance completely correct.

Quickly, I used magic to try and probe the illusion, but to no avail. The image of Nessa didn't even waver.

'How can you do this?' I demanded. 'You have neither seen Nessa nor heard her speak?'

'There are not merely words inside a head!' the witch retorted. 'There are images and sounds – I took all that I needed from your little spy's head. The rest I have been taking from your own mind even as we speak!'

Angered by that, I attempted to slither into her mind. I intended to give her pain – just enough to make a scream. But I could not do it. There was some type of barrier there – one that I could not breach. She was strong.

'I believe that you could indeed enter the arena in that guise and fool the spectators – even the High Mages,' I admitted grudgingly. 'But what makes you think that fighting alongside me would make our victory certain?'

'I am Grimalkin, the assassin of the Malkin clan. I am a witch who can wield powerful magic; more than that, I am skilled in the arts of combat. I could defeat the Haggenbrood alone if necessary.'

I would have laughed at her arrogance, but I did not do so. I had never heard of the Malkin clan, nor of a witch assassin, but this purra radiated utter confidence and certainty. She really believed that she could do it. And had she not already slain four elite guards?

'The real problem would be to get you out of here and back to my quarters before the trial,' I explained. 'These dungeons are very secure. I only managed to reach this level because I can make myself very small, as you have already seen. I can slither through a crack or under a door. Can you do that?'

She shook her head and her whole body shimmered. Once again I was looking at the pointy-toothed purra. 'I can create that illusion, but lack the ability to change my size. If you ease the tightness of the silver chain around my neck I will do the rest. But I still need three things from you in return.'

'Name them,' I said.

'First of all, I want my weapons returned to me. There are ten blades and a pair of special scissors. I also require the straps and sheaths that hold them. Secondly, I require the piece of star ore that was taken from me.'

'It will be difficult enough to seize and return your weapons to you; to get the star-stone will be impossible. It is very valuable and will now be under tight guard.' It had almost certainly been placed in the Plunder Room, the most secure vault in the city.

'I want it. It belongs to me!'

'A purra has no rights of ownership. Cease making that foolish demand and be content with your weapons.'

'Mage,' she said mockingly, 'it was a question of ownership that brought you to the extremely difficult position in which you now find yourself. From your servant I learned how you slew the High Mage and the Shaiksa assassin to win back the three girls into your possession. I know that you are a formidable warrior, thus I offer you the respect that I would deny others. But we come from different races and cultures. In Pendle, where I live, there is no slavery, no ownership of people, and a female *can* own property. Thus we see things from different perspectives. Accept my rights and I will accept yours. And now we come to the third thing that you must bring me. It is a large leather sack that contains something very dangerous. Of the three things that I require to be returned to me, this is the most important.'

'Then you must tell me exactly what it contains.'

'It would be better for you to remain in ignorance, but I can see into your head, mage, and I know that curiosity is your greatest flaw. It was that trait I used within my spell of compulsion to draw you here. If I keep silent, you will meddle anyway. The sack contains the head of the Fiend, the most powerful of all the entities who dwell within the dark.'

Her words puzzled me. I had never heard of anything called the 'Fiend'. Nor did I understand what she meant by the 'dark'. Beyond this world there were domains of the spirits such as Askana, the dwelling place of our gods – but as for Kobalos and human souls, where they went after death was unknown to us. They went up or down, and none returned to tell of their experience – though most suspected it was better to go up than down.

'What is the "dark"?' I asked.

'It is the abode of daemons and gods – and of their servants after death. It is the place we witches return to.'

'Is the head of a god in the sack?' I asked.

'Yes, he could be described as a god. There are many Old Gods and, intact, he is more powerful than all the others combined. The rest of his body is bound far away so the head must remain separate – lest his servants succeed in resurrecting him. His vengeance would be terrible.'

'I know nothing of your gods,' I told the purra. 'We have many. My personal favourite is Cougis, the dog-headed god, but many of my people worship Olkie, the god of Kobalos blacksmiths, who has four iron arms and teeth made of brass. However, the greatest of our gods is called Talkus, which means the God Who Is Yet to Be. He is not yet born but we all eagerly await his arrival.'

The purra called Grimalkin smiled at me, showing her pointed teeth. 'Your people have your truths and my people have ours. We are very different in our beliefs,' she told me. 'I will respect your faith and, in return, I ask that you respect mine. The head in the sack *must* be returned to me. That is the most important thing of all. But whatever you do, leave it within the sack. It would be extremely dangerous to remove it. If you wish to survive, you will need to curb your curiosity.'

'First I must locate it,' I said, then pointed at the twitching rat. 'Release him from your magic so that he can find the sack and the other items that you require.'

The purra nodded, and Hom suddenly stopped quivering and rolled over onto his little ratty feet, his whiskers twitching. I quickly gave him instructions: 'I need the precise location of a number of objects taken from this purra by the Oussa,' I told him. 'The most important of these is a large leather sack. Secondly, find the star-stone. Additionally, there are a number of weapons, and the straps and sheaths that contain them. Report back immediately following the completion of your task!'

He turned, and with an angry flick of his thin tail he left the dungeon.

'How long is it likely to take?' the purra asked.

'Far less time than it will take to obtain what you have asked for. But he will not return here – although he has acute hearing and sharp vision, in that form he lacks the means to speak. So now I must leave and return to my quarters to hear his report from a self that can.'

'Before you go, let us make the terms of the trade clear,' the purra said.

I stared at her in astonishment.

'I know all about the importance of trade to your people,' she continued. 'If you do your utmost to return to me my stolen possessions and enable me to free myself, in return I will help you to slay the Haggenbrood. What is more, once we leave this place I will do nothing to hinder what you consider to be your lawful business. Is it a trade?'

'I need time to reflect upon that. I will consider the possibility.'

'There is little time! Before you go, ease the noose around my neck. Do it now!'

I shook my head. 'No, I cannot do that yet. First I will try to get the items that were taken from you. If I achieve that, I will return and do as you ask.'

I did not yet trust the purra. I needed to consider the

situation more carefully. And, as I told her, I wanted to see if I could retrieve her possessions and thus fulfil my part of the trade.

The brow of the purra furrowed with anger but, without another word, I made myself very small and slithered out under the door.

CHAPTER
16
THE DEAD WITCH

I returned to my quarters as swiftly as possible and waited there for Hom to make his report. Suddenly I felt very un-certain. The proposal made by the purra with pointed teeth had seemed reasonable at the time but now, away from her, I felt foolish.

How could I have allowed myself to negotiate with a mere female like that? Was it skaiium? The same thing had occurred when I'd talked to Nessa and she had pressed her forehead against mine. I had been influenced unduly, and had then recklessly attempted the rescue of the youngest sister, killing a High Mage and a Shaiksa assassin in the process and bringing me to my present situation. Now it was happening again with this strange purra.

Or perhaps she was using some sort of magic to control my thoughts and actions? After all, I knew nothing of this witch and her magic; my usual defences might not be effective.

I took a deep breath and began to focus on the problem, putting aside my fears and attempting to assess the situation logically. There was no doubt that the human witch could create a magical illusion strong enough to pass herself off as Nessa. I had been prepared to release the girl to distract the Haggenbrood momentarily – so why not do the same with this purra? She was the assassin of a witch clan, and to slay four of the Oussa demonstrated that she was a formidable warrior.

I also knew that I could enter her dungeon again undetected, and loosen the noose about her neck – that was all she had asked. I did not understand how she could then escape and reach my quarters in order to accompany me into the arena, but that was her problem. If she failed to do so, I would simply take the three sisters and keep to my original plan.

The homunculus came out of his hole and clambered up onto the chair again.

'Make your report!' I commanded.

'The weapons and the star-stone are in the Plunder Room of the Triumvirate,' Hom announced.

The Plunder Room was accurately named – that was where I had expected the items to have been placed. It was effectively the treasury of the Triumvirate, the place where confiscated goods of special interest or value were stored. It was well-guarded; too well-guarded – virtually impregnable. It would be impossible for me to retrieve the first two items required by the human witch.

'Did you find the location of the leather sack?' I asked.

'It was disposed of – thrown down one of the rubbish chutes.'

'Are you sure?' I asked. How could something considered to be so important by the pointy-toothed purra have been discarded as worthless? I wondered.

'Yes, the sack was opened and found to contain a severed head in such an advanced state of decomposition that it was dumped very quickly.'

'Give me the location of the chute!' I demanded. No doubt the rotting head it contained was an exceedingly loathsome, stinking abomination, but the purra considered it to be the most important of her possessions. Once I explained the impossibility of getting hold of the rest, it might be enough to satisfy her. Retrieving it should not prove difficult.

'District Boktar North, Level Thirteen, chute 179,' Hom replied.

'I will go there immediately. Have one of your selves meet me there and take me directly to the sack.'

It did not take me long to reach chute 179, which was working at full capacity. From above, it had the appearance of a huge concave half-cylinder with an oval hole at its centre. From the pipes overhanging it, all types of refuse were being disgorged into the gaping mouth of the stinking chute: mostly bones, slime, offal and excrement.

The white skoya was covered in yellow-brown slime with clots of green, and I was glad that I did not have to climb down into the chute itself: there was a system of ladders provided for the maintenance workers. Their job, in addition to attending to the pipes and keeping the flow fast and free, was to descend into the area directly beneath the chute and use spades and carts to spread out the refuse. Otherwise the growing mound beneath would eventually block the flow.

I negotiated the series of ladders. Looking down, I could see just one solitary Kobalos pushing a laden cart as he walked away from the flow from the chute. The presence of a haizda mage down here might be reported so I didn't want to be noticed. There might be up to a dozen Kobalos employed at each chute, but each had to move his load some distance away: if I was lucky, no one would see me. Thus I decided to conserve my magic and dispense with the cloaking spell.

Hom was waiting obediently at the foot of the ladder, his thin rat-tail twitching energetically. Without waiting to be told, he immediately scampered away and I followed, trudging through the muck and getting my boots dirty. It wasn't long before we reached our objective. Finding it was easy; the problem was that someone had got there first. There were two figures in the distance, and one was holding the sack. They were engaged in conversation, and at first they did not notice my approach.

But when I was within about twenty paces of them, the one with the sack spun round to face me.

To my astonishment, I saw that it was a purra, but not one from Valkarky – she was a stranger. Unlike the one with pointed teeth, she wore a skirt that came down to her ankles, with a dirty fox-fur jacket buttoned at the neck. She was barefoot, with slime squelching up between her toes, and her face was twisted with hatred.

I wondered if they were accomplices of Grimalkin – other human witches. If so, might they have similar magical powers and fighting abilities?

'Drop the sack and go!' I commanded. 'You have no business in our city, but you may keep your lives.'

The other purra was some distance behind the first and I couldn't see her clearly, but I heard her cackle with laughter at my words.

The nearer purra threw the sack to one side, drew a knife and began to stride towards me, a purposeful expression on her face. She began to mutter under her breath, and I realized that she was indeed a human witch and was trying to use magic against me. Within seconds her appearance changed dramatically. Her tongue protruded about an arm's length from her mouth; it was forked like that of a snake. Next her face twisted into something bestial: large fangs grew down over her bottom lip, almost reaching her chin, and her hair became a nest of writhing snakes.

I was not sure what the purpose of the transformation was. Perhaps it was intended to distract me in some way. There was no doubt in my mind that the witch had become marginally uglier than before, but it did not affect my concentration in the slightest.

I stepped backwards, focused my mind, and before the knife came within range of my body, I drew my sabre and struck her head clean from her shoulders. She collapsed in a heap, blood spurting from the stump of her neck. I kicked the head away and prepared to face the second witch.

This one approached me slowly. She was cackling again as if she found the whole business highly amusing. 'I can keep my life, can I?' she crowed. 'And what life would that be?'

For a moment I did not understand her meaning, but she was closer now, less than ten paces away, and I could smell loam, rot and dead flesh. The matted hair was crusted with dried mud and I could see maggots wriggling within it. Then something writhed and slowly emerged from her left ear. It was a fat, grey earthworm.

I focused my hearing on her and concentrated. She was wheezing slightly but not breathing in any natural way, and there was no heartbeat. It could mean only one thing.

She was correct: she had no life. She was already dead.

She attacked, running directly towards me, hands outstretched, claws ready to rend my flesh.

I am fast but the dead witch was faster. Her sudden attack took me by surprise, and the claws of her right hand missed my eye by a whisker.

Her left hand didn't miss, though. It clamped hard upon my

own left wrist. I tried to pull it free but the grip tightened. Never had I encountered such strength. I punched her in the face with my free hand but she didn't even flinch. Her fingers were like a tightening metal band cutting through flesh to squeeze the bone. My numbed hand released the sabre and it fell into the slime.

I was a mage who had studied the occult for many years. However, I had no experience at all of entities that could function in bodies that were essentially dead. In that moment I realized how big a place the world was and how much I had yet to learn. We Kobalos have a history of fighting humans, but we believe them to be far more numerous than us. It is perhaps fortunate that they are divided into many conflicting kingdoms, but we have little knowledge of any who use magic in those more distant places. Thus I knew nothing of human witches and their powers. How, I wondered, could I kill something that was already dead?

I drew a dagger with my free hand and plunged it into the

witch's throat. It had no effect, and again her claws lunged towards my face. I spun away, still gripped by the witch, our bodies stretched taut.

Then I brought logic to bear upon the situation. I whirled the dagger across in a fast arc. The blade cut straight through the witch's wrist, severing it from her body. She fell backwards into the slime, leaving her left hand behind, still gripping my wrist. But it began to twitch and slowly relax its hold, and it was the work of a moment to pull it off and cast it aside. By the time the dead witch had regained her feet, the sabre was back in my left hand and I was ready.

I had no choice but to cut her into pieces. How else could I terminate her attack?

Soon she had no arms or legs and could not even crawl. There was no blood – just a trickle of vile black fluid. To be sure, I sliced off her head, and held it up by the hair. Her eyes gazed back at me, full of fury, and her lips twitched as if she would speak. In disgust, I flung her head as far away as possible. Then I picked up the leather sack, retrieved my sabre, wiping it clean on the torso of the dismembered witch, and went back towards the ladder with Hom scampering at my heels.

Soon I was safely back in my quarters. First I checked on the three sisters. They were sleeping with their arms around each other.

Next I examined the sack and weighed it carefully in my hands. It was certainly extremely large. I remembered the warning given by the witch with pointed teeth, but I was curious to see such a head – that of the most powerful of their gods. Also, despite the report given to me by Hom, the head did not stink. So I undid the string and reached inside.

I felt something sharp; something made of bone – two coiled objects. I peered into the sack. They were horns. This was a horned god. One of our own horned gods was called Unktus, but he was a relatively minor deity worshipped only by the lowest menials of the city. I lifted the head out of the sack, put it on the chair opposite me and studied it carefully.

No wonder they had chosen it to be the chief of their gods. It was much more impressive than depictions of Unktus in the grottoes of worship. There was no sign of putrefaction, and the horns were not unlike those of a ram. Once it had surely been lordly and handsome despite its close approximation to the human form. However, it had been cruelly mutilated. One eye was missing and the other stitched shut. The mouth was stuffed with brambles and nettles.

My curiosity satisfied, I was about to return it to the sack when the stitched lids over the remaining eye twitched. Immediately I heard a deep groan. The sound did not emanate from the head, but from the floor beneath the chair. That was odd – could it be that the head was still conscious? And perhaps the essence of the god was not just confined to its head? In some entities consciousness can be diffuse and not merely trapped within the flesh.

The mouth was being forced open by the nettles and brambles, so I began to tug them out, dropping them onto the floor beneath the chair. I then saw further evidence of violence: the teeth had been smashed; only yellow stumps remained. As I tugged out the last of the bramble twigs, there was another groan. This time it came from the mouth, not the floor.

The jaw began to move and the lips to tremble. At first all that came out was a sigh and a croak, but then the head spoke clearly and eloquently.

'I forgive you for what you did to my servants. It was understandable as they were interlopers in your city. But do as I say now and I will reward you beyond your wildest dreams. Disobey me and I will inflict upon you an eternity of pain!'

I took a deep breath to calm myself and took stock of the situation before replying. Perhaps the witch had been correct and I had been foolish to open the sack and subject myself to unnecessary risk. She was certainly right about my curiosity, though. It was part of what I was. Sometimes danger had to be faced in order to gain knowledge. I knew I must be bold and face down this maimed god.

'You are in no position to reward anyone,' I told the head. 'I have been informed that you were once a powerful god but are now helpless. It must be difficult for one so high and mighty to have been brought so low.'

Then, before the mutilated god could bother me further with its threats, I thrust the nettles and brambles back into the mouth and returned the head to the sack.

Once again I visited District Yaksa Central, Level Thirteen, cell forty-two.

I made myself very small and slithered under the dungeon door. I looked up and met the malevolent gaze of the human witch, then quickly grew until we were looking at each other eye to eye.

'Did you retrieve my property?' she asked coldly.

'I have the leather sack with the severed head of your god,' I told her. 'It is back in my quarters. Additionally, I know the location of your blades and the star-stone, but you'll have to manage without them. They are in the most secure place in the city. But these' – I placed two of my own blades on the floor before her – 'may serve you just as well.'

'Do we have a trade?' she asked.

'Yes, it is a trade. You have my word.'

Thus the bargain was struck and I was pleased. Fighting alongside the witch, I would have a real chance against the Haggenbrood. But there were obstacles yet to be overcome. Could she really complete her escape and make her way safely to my quarters?

'Well, mage, I thank you for the loan of the blades, and you have the head – that's the most important thing. To begin with, all you have to do is ease the tightness of the chain about my neck.'

'I can do more than that.' And I released her from the chain so that now she was held only by the four silver pins.

She smiled, showing her pointed teeth. 'Thank you,' she said. 'The only further thing that I require is a guide to take me to my other possessions. Send me the busybody rat.'

'Put such thoughts from your mind!' I said angrily. 'They are in the Plunder Room of the Triumvirate. Any attempt to penetrate that stronghold will result in your certain death.'

'The "Triumvirate" – that sounds very grand. What is it?'

'It is the ruling body of Valkarky, composed of the three most powerful High Mages in the city.'

'No doubt replacements will be found if anything untoward were to happen to them. I would hate to see such a fine city without proper governance,' she said, her voice filled with sarcasm. 'Send me the little rat! Will you do it? Then I will stand by your side in the arena. Go now! It would be wise to be well clear of this dungeon before I escape.'

Filled with anger at her presumption, I made myself small and left the cell.

Once back in my quarters, I seethed with anger at her foolishness. But as the trial approached, I found myself growing more desperate. So I summoned Hom and ordered him to send one of his rat-selves to guide the witch.

No doubt it was futile. I did not see how she could even free herself from the silver pins, let alone storm the Plunder Room.

I blew myself up to my favourite fighting size, which was a head taller than Nessa, and made my preparations. First I brushed my long thick black overcoat – something I would not entrust to a servant – and polished its thirteen bone buttons. The sabre I thrust into my belt; my two favourite newly sharpened blades went into the scabbards on my chest. A third dagger I hid in my coat pocket.

After about half an hour the homunculus scurried out of his

hole and clambered up onto the chair to face me. He seemed somewhat breathless, and his brow was flushed with excitement.

'There is news!' he exclaimed. 'The purra escaped and then breached the defences of the Plunder Room. One of the Triumvirate is dead!'

I looked at Hom in astonishment. How had she managed to do such a thing? 'Where is the witch now?' I demanded.

'Gone, master. The murderess fled Valkarky and is heading south. A large band of Oussa has been sent after her with orders to catch her quickly but kill her slowly.'

I was filled with anger. No doubt she had always planned to make her escape. She had used me. I had been a fool to trust her. And why had she not taken the head of the horned god with her? She had claimed it was important to her. No doubt she had lied about that too.

It was time to go and wake up Nessa and her sisters. In less than an hour we had to face the teeth and claws of the Haggenbrood.

As I stepped into the corridor between the two rooms, I suddenly sensed danger and reached for my sabre.

'Sheathe your blade, mage,' said a voice that I recognized. 'Save it for the arena!'

The witch assassin stepped out of the shadows and smiled widely at me, showing her full set of pointed teeth. She was wearing leather straps which crisscrossed her body, and in the attached scabbards she carried her blades. 'Where is the leather sack?' she demanded.

'It is safe,' I told her.

'Safe?! Nothing is safe in this city. I opened your most secure vault with ease and took what was mine. What I have done, others can emulate. I have human enemies – witches and mages who serve the Fiend. It is only a matter of time before they follow me here!'

'Two witches have been here already. They had the sack in their possession when I encountered them. I killed the live one and chopped the dead witch into six pieces. She is somewhat inconvenienced and poses no threat.'

'Then you have done well, mage. But there will be others. They will never stop. Show me the sack.'

I led her back into the room and handed her the leather bag. She quickly opened it, peered inside and sniffed three times. She did not draw forth the god's head.

'Now leave me alone for a few moments. I need to hide this from prying eyes.'

Her words offended me. Had we not made a trade that meant we were allies? I pushed the affront to the back of my mind. The room was sparsely furnished with just a couch, two chairs and a table. There was nowhere the sack could be hidden unless she used magic. I did as she requested and returned five minutes later.

'Try and find it,' she said softly.

I tried briefly but without success, using a little of my magic. That did not mean that, given enough time, I could not employ more and discover its whereabouts. But it was well-hidden by her powerful magic. I was impressed.

'It would not be found easily,' I admitted. 'I did not expect to see you again and thought you had deceived me. Reports say that you have escaped the city and are being pursued by the Oussa.'

'We have a trade. Like you, I always keep my word. I promised to aid you in the arena and, yes, I will fight alongside you. It was easy to lay a false trail. And now to business – when do we face the Haggenbrood?'

'Within the hour. We need to tell the eldest of the three sisters that you will be replacing her.'

'Yes, I would like to talk to all three girls – we are humans and alien to this city. I would like to reassure them that all will be well, so I must speak to them alone.'

'If you wish. It is customary to keep one's purrai in separate rooms but as a special concession, because of the danger we will soon face, I have allowed them to be together. Come. I will take you to them.'

CHAPTER 18
A VERY INTERESTING QUESTION

❧NESSA❧

I had been doing my best to console Susan and Bryony, but they were scared and tearful. As a result it was a long time before I could bring myself to tell them something of what they faced in the arena. I felt like crying too, but what good would that do? So I bit my bottom lip hard to stop it from trembling and said what had to be said.

'Once there, we are to be bound to stakes,' I began. It was better to forewarn them, so that they could prepare themselves.

'What did you say? We are going to be tied to stakes?' Susan said, her pretty face twisting in alarm. 'And watched by an audience of those beasts?'

I nodded. 'It is the way things are done here. It would be a good idea to keep your eyes tight closed so you don't have to see what happens. But it won't be for long – Slither will slay his enemies quickly. You've seen how he fights. Then it will be over and you'll be cut free. Soon we'll be on our way to our aunt and uncle's and all will be well. This will just seem like a very bad dream.'

'All won't be well if you can't stay with us, Nessa,' Bryony said, her voice wobbly with emotion.

'We can only hope that one day I'll be free and able to return to you,' I told them, doing my best to sound confident. 'Somehow I'll find a way to escape so that we can be together again, don't you fear.'

For all my brave words, it seemed likely that we'd all be dead very soon. Even if by some miracle we survived the arena, there would be no safe haven in our aunt and uncle's house for me. The beast would sell me in the slave market. That's if he didn't kill me himself first. I'd seen the way he looked at all three of us. He was finding it increasingly difficult not to sink his teeth into our throats.

I heard footsteps and we all turned towards the door. In walked Slither, but he was not alone. To my astonishment he was accompanied by a human; a tall, fierce woman was by his side. Her body was crisscrossed with leather straps holding sheathed blades, and her skirt was divided and strapped to her thighs. Was this another of the fierce slaves that we'd encountered in the tower? What was she doing here? Why had Slither allowed her to enter his quarters? I wondered.

That was bad enough. Then she smiled and I saw that her cruel mouth was filled with sharp pointed teeth. I took a step backwards, startled and afraid. Both Susan and Bryony ran behind me.

'This is Grimalkin and she is here to help us,' Slither said. 'She is a witch, and one of your people.'

He left us without saying anything more. We were alone with the woman, and for a moment or two she simply stared into my eyes. Was the beast telling the truth? Was this strange woman really here to help us? And if so, how?

She pointed to the floor. 'Let us sit and talk,' she said. 'We have much to discuss.'

Why was she here? What could there be to talk about with this fearsome stranger?

There were five chairs in the room but she sat down cross-legged on the floor, then looked up at us and beckoned. 'We have little time. Sit now!'

There was command in her voice – she seemed like someone who was used to getting her own way, so we sat down on the floor facing her. Susan began to cry softly but the woman ignored her.

'Tell me what happened and how you came to be in the possession of Slither,' she demanded, staring hard at me. 'Tell me also what you hope for in the future.'

I did as she asked, beginning with my father's death and the trade that he had made with Slither.

'So you are to be sold in the slave market but your

two sisters are to go free? How do you feel about that?'

'Better that than all three of us dying,' I replied. 'But I would also like to join my sisters at my aunt and uncle's house. The life of a slave is brutal. I have seen the cuts the beasts inflict upon them.'

'Now tell me about your journey here.'

While my sisters looked on in silence, I gave a full account of our visit to the tower and how we had escaped. After a brief description of Slither's fight with the horse creature, I told her of our terror on arriving at Valkarky.

'Without doubt this Kobalos called Slither is a formidable warrior,' the witch said. 'I will fight alongside him in the arena and then you will be free to leave this city.'

'Will that be allowed?' I asked.

'What they don't know *will* hurt them,' she said with a grim smile. 'Nessa, I will take your place in the arena.'

I opened my mouth, but before I could get the words out there was a shimmer in the air, and the body and face of the witch became strangely blurred. Then, to my utter astonishment, I was staring at myself. It was as though I were looking into a mirror. Bryony and Susan both gasped and their eyes flicked back and forth between me and the transformed Grimalkin.

Seconds later, there was another shimmer and the witch was there again, glaring back at us. 'Now do you see how it may be accomplished?'

All three of us nodded. I was too stunned to speak.

'She became just like you, Nessa!' Bryony suddenly

exclaimed, finding her tongue. 'She could have been your identical twin.'

'But it's magic!' Susan protested. 'It's wrong to do such things. No good can come of it.'

'No?' asked the witch. 'Would you rather die in the arena, then?'

Susan didn't answer. She looked down at the floor and started weeping again.

'I will do my best to slay the Haggenbrood and to protect your two sisters,' the witch continued, staring straight into my eyes. 'I'll also do my best to ensure that all three of you stay together and are taken to live with your relatives. I do not promise that it will happen. But I will try.'

'Thank you,' I said, forcing a smile onto my face. For the first time in days I felt a glimmer of hope. For some reason, fearsome as she was, I trusted this witch. 'Will I stay here while you take my place?'

'Yes,' Grimalkin answered. 'As I understand it, these are private quarters and no one would think to enter without permission from a haizda mage. And why should they suspect anything, anyway? You will be safe here. And now,' she continued, 'I would like to ask you a question. They enslave human females whom they call purrai. Most are the daughters of slaves who are born here in captivity. Others, very much the minority, are captured and enslaved. But I have seen no sign at all of their own females. Why are they hidden away?'

'We haven't seen their women, either,' I admitted. 'On their city thoroughfares there are only male Kobalos and the occasional purra being dragged about like an animal on a leash. I am sorry but I am unable to answer your question.'

The witch nodded. 'But it is a very interesting question nonetheless,' she mused. 'I suspect that when we learn the answer, we will understand these creatures far better.'

CHAPTER
~19~
HOSTILE, HUNGRY EYES

On first glimpsing the witch, the three sisters were terrified and shrank away as if she were some kind of fearsome monster. I found it difficult to understand. The four of them were human, after all. But when I returned half an hour later, they had calmed down somewhat and the four were engaged in conversation.

Nessa in particular seemed much happier, and I wondered if they had been plotting together. Perhaps the witch did not respect a trade in the same way that I did? It made little difference. The priority now was to survive our encounter with the Haggenbrood. I would deal with any other difficulties later.

Grimalkin had explained to them what needed to be done, and Nessa seemed calm and agreeable to being replaced in the arena. It appeared that she had entrusted the safety of her two sisters to the assassin. I wondered what the witch had said to win them over so completely.

The three sisters hugged each other as we left for the arena. All three were crying as Grimalkin used her magic to mask herself as Nessa.

As they pulled apart, I was surprised to see that Susan was the calmest and least affected of them all. She wiped away her tears, straightened her back and forced a smile onto her face as she looked directly at Nessa. 'I'm sorry for being such a burden and for always complaining,' she told her. 'If I live through this I'll try to be a better sister in future.'

'You'll be back soon,' Nessa promised. 'You'll both live, I promise you, and we'll all be safe again.'

I wondered if the girl was right. But I could not dwell on the question for long: it was time to face the Haggenbrood.

The arena was already full of excited spectators who began calling out and jeering, baying for our blood the moment we entered. News of my trial had spread throughout Valkarky and, to say the least, the crowd were hostile towards me. Because we are outsiders, and our lives and vocation, gathering power, managing our haizdas and seeking understanding of the universe, are mysterious and unknown to the majority, haizda mages have never been popular in the city. To make matters worse, I had slain a High Mage, one of those who might one day have become part of the Triumvirate. Valkarky is very patriarchal; in their minds I had slain one of the city fathers. During the trial, as the hysteria increased, it would become more personal still – as if each spectator believed that I had killed his *own* father.

Of course, many had come simply to view the spectacle and savour the spilling of red blood on the arena floor, as I had done as a youngster. Some were visibly salivating already.

On being led into position, all three girls looked terrified and sobbed hysterically. It was hard to believe that the real Nessa had been left behind in my quarters. It was a testament to the power of the human witch. A haizda mage must gather knowledge wherever he can – from friend and foe alike. Should I survive this encounter, I intended to learn from this witch assassin.

The purrai were tied to the posts by the Kobalos who served the trial judge while I waited patiently close to the pit where the Haggenbrood was confined. I glanced down through the grille. Nothing was moving. The creature was sedated. The moment the grille was removed, the first of three trumpets would sound and the creature would become aware, wishing to know more of the opponent it faced. At the second trumpet it would crawl out of the pit. The blast of the third trumpet would rouse it to extreme fury and blood-lust, and the battle would begin. Such was its conditioning. It was all very predictable – up to that point. But once the battle began, everything was uncertain.

During my earlier preparations in my quarters I had gone into a trance to summon into my mind all previous trials during the last fifty years. The Haggenbrood had proved victorious in all three hundred and twelve encounters, never once repeating the same pattern of attack. Most victories had been achieved within less than a minute.

Dressed in his black robes of office, the trial judge entered the arena and held up both hands for silence. He had to wait several minutes before the crowd calmed down sufficiently for the proceedings to begin.

In a loud voice he began to read out the charges:

'The haizda mage known as Slither is charged with the murder of the High Mage known as Nunc and stealing from him the three purrai that you see before you.'

At this a great roar of anger erupted from the spectators and the judge had to hold up his hand to order silence again.

'Secondly he is charged with the unlawful slaying of a Shaiksa assassin who attempted to prevent him from leaving with the stolen purrai. Thirdly he is charged with the unlawful slaying of the hyb warrior who was sent to execute him for those crimes.'

The spectators brayed out their anger once more, and the judge was forced to hold up his hand even longer to command order. Only when absolute silence was achieved did he continue.

'The haizda mage refutes those charges on the grounds that the three purrai were, and still are, his property and that he killed lawfully to protect his rights. In addition, his mind has been probed thoroughly and he is convinced that he is being truthful. He would therefore have been released but for the fact that the Shaiksa Brotherhood has objected on the grounds of evidence supplied to them from the dying mind of the assassin slain by this haizda mage.

'That communication asserts that Lord Nunc had paid Slither for the purrai and they were his lawful property. Lord Nunc is dead and therefore unavailable for questioning. Consequently, as this contradiction is impossible to resolve, we require this trial by combat.'

Then the judge pointed at me.

The auditorium had been absolutely quiet during the final part of the reading of the charge. Now he called out dramatically in a voice filled with authority, loud enough to reach every corner of the arena. 'Choose!' he cried.

I was being asked to choose my starting position. This had to be directly in front of one of the three posts. I had, of course, selected it long before entering the arena. I quickly stood before the semblance of Nessa. In my possession I had the sabre, which I now drew, preparing for battle. In addition I now had three blades; the extra one in my pocket was for the witch, even though I knew that behind the facade she projected, she had her own blades too. It was important for the maintenance of the magical illusion that the spectators see me hand her a blade.

The employment of magic such as cloaking or changing size were forbidden in the arena. I hoped the witch's use of it would go undetected. Otherwise I would instantly be declared the loser and my life – and those of the sisters – would be forfeit.

The judge signalled again by raising his arms. This time three Kobalos appeared. Together they walked towards the heavy grille and, in a well-rehearsed move, lifted it clear and carried it away, strutting self-importantly across the arena. Now the dark mouth of the pit was wide open.

The judge walked to each side of the triangular arena in turn, and bowed to the spectators ostentatiously. His fourth bow was to me – to the one who was about to die. And with that a low murmuring began, gathering slowly in volume.

I returned his bow and then straightened up again, maintaining eye-contact until he looked away. Then he left the arena and raised his hand high above his head. In answer to that gesture a loud trumpet blast was heard. It filled the auditorium, echoing from wall to wall.

At that sound, the several thousand spectators became absolutely silent again. At first, all that could be heard was the irritating sniffing of the youngest sister.

But then the Haggenbrood spoke to me from the darkness of the pit.

There came a crepitation, a rhythmical clicking and snapping that somehow seemed to be full of meaning; it was almost like speech, as if a withered old Kobalos had opened and closed his arthritic jaws while his bewildered mind searched the empty vault of his thoughts for fragments of memory. Then the noises sharpened into focus and became words that all present could hear and understand.

It spoke in Losta, the language used by Kobalos and humans. The voice had three distinct components which, even as I listened, fused so fully into one that they could not be separated; all three of the creature's selves were speaking to me simultaneously, three mouths opening; one thinking mind teasing, taunting and testing the fibre of my resolve.

'*You are a haizda mage,*' it said. '*It is a long time since I last tasted one of your kind.*'

'Talk not of eating. You have had your last meal!' I cried. 'Tonight I will carve your flesh into cubes and feed it to the carrion creatures in the sewers of the city. Then I will melt your bones in the furnaces so that they can be used for glue. Nothing will be wasted! You will prove a useful servant until the end!'

In response to my words the crowd gave a roar of approval. But I did not fool myself into thinking that they were now on my side. It was just the opposite – they were looking forward to my bloody defeat. But my words had given them hope that I would make a proper fight of it; that the spectacle would not be over quite as quickly as was the norm.

'*You speak boldly, but soon you will start to scream, haizda mage. I will bite off your arms and legs, and lick the stumps to stop the flow of blood. Then I will give you a slow, painful death so that all can delight in your screams. Finally I will slice the soft flesh of your purrai very slowly, savouring each morsel.*'

Hearing those words, all three captives became even more hysterical, straining against their ties in vain, but I did not reply. We had talked enough. Action would speak much louder than words.

Then came the second trumpet blast. In the following silence I heard the Haggenbrood begin to move. As the creature dragged itself out of the pit, I registered a razor-beak and two murderously sharp-clawed hands. Within seconds, the first of the selves had emerged and was regarding me with hostile, hungry eyes.

I had never been so close to the unconfined Haggenbrood before, and it momentarily filled me with dismay. It was even more formidable than I had imagined. Despite the fact that each part of it had only four appendages and a long serpentine neck, they resembled nothing more than insects. Glistening as if smeared with some gelatinous substance, the sides and arms were covered in plates of bone like the ribbed armour worn in battle by Kobalos High Mages. It gave off a new stench now. I smelled its hunger and eagerness for battle.

I took a deep breath, straightened my back and gathered my courage. I was a haizda mage, an undefeated warrior. I would prevail.

Within moments its three selves were crouched on all fours, ready to spring, but they could not do so until the blast of the third trumpet was heard.

I prepared myself to cut the bonds of the human witch and thrust the blade into her hands as she had asked. I was reaching for it, but suddenly, at the last moment, I changed my mind and left it in my pocket – with good reason too.

Chapter 20
The Tawny Death

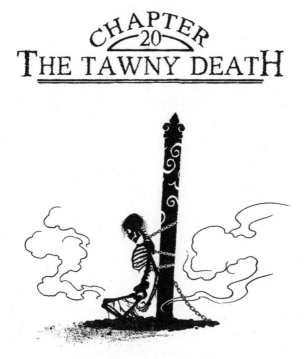

Out of the previous trial encounters that I had studied, on only two occasions had the Haggenbrood concentrated its efforts on its opponent, waiting to attack and devour the sacrificial purrai until after he was dead.

In both cases the opponent had somehow managed to inflict the first wound on the Haggenbrood. In neither case had the trial lasted long, but the move had succeeded in changing the pattern of conflict. If I could get it to concentrate solely on me, then the intervention of the witch would be an even more effective surprise.

As the sound of the third trumpet echoed from the walls of the auditorium, the twelve limbs of the Haggenbrood extended, and the three selves each came up onto two legs, growling with battle-fury. Then it attacked. I was the target, not the purrai.

But a fraction of a second later I began to move too – directly towards it. In my left hand I held Old Rowler's sabre; in my right my favourite dagger.

Five strides, each faster than its predecessor, brought me to the edge of the pit and within cutting range of my multi-selved opponent. The element of surprise was now mine. It had not expected me to be so bold. Teeth snapped towards me. Hot foul breath was in my face. Talons missed my face by the thickness of a rat's whisker.

Then it was my turn.

I attempted two blows, one fractionally after the other. The scything cut with my sabre missed because of the amazingly rapid reaction of the self I'd targeted; my favourite dagger didn't.

Its tip penetrated an eye. The crowd roared. Three throats gave a simultaneous delicious scream. Each self felt the pain. That was good to know.

Now the Haggenbrood only had five eyes left.

Then I leaped across the pit, landing safely on the other side. My tail was parallel with my back and ready. I needed it for balance.

The selves scuttled towards me, jaws open wide, faces twisted in fury. But they didn't leap over the pit. They kept to the edges – two on my left, one on my right. I waited until the very last moment, then did a back-flip, returning to the opposite side. Quickly I ran towards the post where the witch in the shape of Nessa was secured, and cut her bonds.

As I handed her the blade, a huge gasp went up from the crowd. This had never been done before, but there was no mention of it in the rules. It was perfectly legal.

We stood side by side facing the pit. Once again the three selves of the Haggenbrood circled it slowly, five eyes signalling their fierce intent.

Sometimes in battle we act instinctively. The thrust of a blade, the avoidance of a spear is automatic and faster than thought. One enters a trance-like condition in which the body moves of its own volition, far faster than any action can be planned.

So it was now. And there was something else: when I fought alongside the witch, it was as if we shared one consciousness. Whether she employed some human magic to achieve that, or whether, in the heat of battle, we somehow became transcendent, elevated to a fighting ferocity where our two bodies were controlled by one joint mind, I didn't know. But it seemed to me that the way we two fought was similar to the Haggenbrood's coordinated selves.

My concentration was total and I no longer heard the baying of the excited crowd. I fought with Grimalkin in a pocket of silence.

One touch was enough to cause kirrhos, the tawny death, but as we attacked, taking the battle to the Haggenbrood, its claws missed my face by inches. I felt its collective corrosive breath singe the skin of my face, but our blades flashed and the creature screamed. We cut it and it bled.

I was aware of Grimalkin's cuts and thrusts as if they were my own; no doubt she too felt my strikes at the enemy that confronted us. It was as if I were floating just above my body, watching us do battle below. I remember briefly wondering how the fight appeared to the spectators on their tiers of seats. Surely they would not see it as I did?

For how could the purra, Nessa, fight with such consummate ferocity and skill? Somehow the witch must be cloaking that from their gaze, making it seem as if the brunt of the battle was all mine. In truth, it was hard for me to judge which of us made the greater contribution. As I said, we were like one. My arms were her arms; her blades were my blades. It was a pleasure to share combat with such a warrior.

Within moments two of the Haggenbrood's selves had been cut to pieces, their body parts scattered across the arena floor. Victory was almost ours, but then, with victory almost in sight, there was a small reversal of fortune.

The last of the enemy selves broke away from us and scuttled straight towards Susan, the elder of the two bound sisters. This took me completely by surprise: the creature had hitherto shown no interest in the captives, who had their eyes shut in terror. The creature was defeated, and could not have achieved anything by such an act unless it could slay both purrai – but it would not have time for that. Perhaps it was sheer spitefulness.

I intercepted it, slaying it on the spot by burying a blade deep within its left eye. It twitched, jerked and went into a death spasm. Seconds later all life had left its body! We had defeated the Haggenbrood. I had won!

My unexpected victory caused an uproar which came close to a riot. Over a hundred stewards rushed in, and immediately set about the foolish spectators with clubs and maces. I watched heads break and bleed as the stewards laid about them, clearly enjoying their task. Soon more blood flowed there than had ever graced the combat area itself. It was enjoyable to watch and I savoured every moment. But all too soon the unruly spectators had been forced back into their seats.

After order had been restored and the bodies removed, the trial judge climbed up into the arena and formally announced my win. He did not look happy at my unexpected and un-orthodox triumph. I could see that he was struggling to conceal his shock and dismay. But what could he do other than confirm my victory?

This time he did not read aloud. No doubt he had prepared only one statement – that announcing my expected defeat and death. But he spoke slowly and ponderously, as if weighing each phrase in his mind before uttering it.

'The haizda mage who stands before you has triumphed in combat and proven his case beyond refute. Both the Shaiksa Brotherhood and the Triumvirate must acknowledge and abide by this outcome. He is free to leave the city and may take his purrai with him. They are now officially his lawful property. That is the law and none are above it.'

All that remained was for me to seize my property, return to my quarters and leave as soon as possible. I cut the youngest purra, Bryony, free, but when I approached the stake to which Susan was bound, I suddenly realized what had happened.

As I'd intercepted the third self of the Haggenbrood, unknown to me, the tip of its claw must have penetrated the skin on Susan's forearm. That had sealed her fate. Her skin had become yellow-brown in colour and as dry as ancient parchment. Her face was distorted and she was gurgling deep in her throat, obviously in the grip of terrible pain. Even as I reached her, she took her dying breath, a great rattling sob. I could do nothing to help her. There is no antidote, no cure for kirrhos.

The youngest sister screamed in horror and grief as, within seconds, Susan's eyes fell back into her skull and her skin began to flake and crack. Within that crust of skin her flesh had melted like soft yellow butter, and her tissues began to ooze out of the widening rifts in her skin, dissolving, dripping down her bones to form a noxious stinking puddle at her feet.

She had succumbed to the tawny death.

CHAPTER 21
THE SLARINDA

❧NESSA❧

I was in Slither's quarters, my thoughts in turmoil, end-
lessly pacing back and forth across the small room
allocated to me. The door was locked, and would remain so
until their return.

I remembered the arena and how Slither had graphically
described what might happen. I saw in my mind's eye the
terrible Haggenbrood holding the grille with a taloned hand.
Slither had stamped upon it and treated the creature with
disdain, but it had never been defeated in previous trials.
How would the mage fare when all three selves attacked him
in the arena?

And what of Grimalkin, the witch assassin? She was formidable and had dark magic at her disposal. She was so confident too – so very sure of herself. But if the Haggenbrood proved victorious, then my sisters would both die.

I heard footsteps approaching Slither's quarters, and the voices of the beast and the witch. Then a child crying. It sounded like poor Bryony. She must have been traumatized by the events in the arena, but despite that, my heart soared with joy. They were here. They had triumphed, surely . . . Otherwise they would be dead. They had won, and soon we would be able to leave this cursed city!

Then the key turned in the lock and the door of my room was opened wide. I stepped out to look at each of them in turn. Suddenly my heart sank.

Where was Susan?

'I did my best, little Nessa,' Slither said, and for the first time he was unable to meet my gaze, 'but your poor sister succumbed to the terrible tawny death. Her brain turned to mush, her eyes fell back into her skull and her flesh slid from her bones. The pain was terrible, but she is at peace now. We must be thankful for that.'

'What?' I cried. 'What do you mean? Where is Susan?'

'She is dead, as I have tried to explain. One fatality was a small price to pay for such a glorious victory – surely you agree that it is better than all of us being dead.'

'But you promised!' I said, my throat and chest tightening

186

so that I could hardly breathe. 'You promised my father to keep my sisters safe!'

'I did my best, Nessa, but the odds against us were great. I could do no more than what I did.'

Tears sprang from my eyes and I fell to my knees beside the sobbing Bryony and held her close. I felt betrayed. I had sacrificed myself just as my father had demanded, but for what?

'Say nothing more,' Grimalkin said to Slither. 'Your words do not help.'

I was aware of their footsteps fading as they retreated to the far corner of the large room, leaving Bryony and me alone in our pocket of misery.

I was in two places at once – my imagination recreating the horror of poor Susan's death; the other part of my mind listening to the conversation between Slither and the witch, which was still just audible to me.

'The two surviving girls *both* deserve to be taken south to live in peace with their relatives,' I heard Grimalkin say. She was a witch, but it was good that she took our side.

'I will keep my promise regarding the younger purra,' Slither replied. 'But I intend to sell Nessa in the slave market, as is my right. After all, she belongs to me. She is my chattel. I must abide by the law of Bindos or become an outlaw. Records are kept, and after my triumph in the arena my notoriety will guarantee that I am closely watched. The High Mages will seize upon any excuse to bring me down. So do you intend to hinder me?'

I looked up and saw the witch shake her head. 'We made a trade and I will keep to it. I always keep my word. But where is the slave market of which you speak?'

'It is held within the large kulad called Karpotha, seventy leagues directly southwest of Valkarky, in the foothills of the Dendar Mountains.'

'Does it hold many slaves?'

'It is the largest of all our purrai markets, but the numbers vary according to the season. The end of winter heralds the first of the auctions. In about a week's time the first big spring market will be held there. Hundreds of purrai will be sold and bought within its walls before being taken in chains back to Valkarky.'

Grimalkin was silent for almost a minute and seemed to be deep in thought. At last she spoke again. 'Where do your own women dwell?' she asked. 'Within the walls of your city I found no trace of them.'

I saw the look of dismay on Slither's face, and he seemed to stagger as if the question had shocked him to the core of his being.

'We Kobalos do not talk of such things,' he replied, clearly outraged. 'To ask such a question is a flagrant breach of etiquette.'

'But I am an outsider,' Grimalkin replied. 'One foreign to your customs and beliefs. So I ask you to answer my question so that I may learn.'

'I too would like an answer!' I called angrily across the room. 'You are hiding something – I feel sure of it!'

Slither glanced quickly towards me, but his answer was directed at Grimalkin. 'Our females were called *Slarinda*; they have been extinct for over three thousand years.'

'Extinct? How could that happen? And how do you continue your species without females?' she demanded.

Slither answered her second question first. 'Kobalos males are born of purrai – human females held prisoner in the skleech pens.'

The witch nodded. 'Why did the Slarinda all die?' she persisted.

'It is a tale of madness, of a time when our whole people must have become temporarily insane. All our women were executed in a vast arena; once its inner doors were shut fast, it could be flooded. And on that day of madness it was flooded with blood.'

'What?! You murdered all your women?' I screamed out, clutching the sobbing Bryony even tighter. 'What manner of filthy beasts are you?'

I saw Slither's tail quiver upright against his back, as it sometimes did when he was annoyed or faced danger. But he didn't so much as glance in my direction. It was as if I had not spoken.

'The Kobalos females were dragged in groups down the steps,' he said slowly. 'Their throats were cut and they were suspended from chains that hung from the high roof of the stadium – until all the blood had drained out of their bodies, pooling upon the ice of the arena floor. It did not freeze, for warm air blew from conduits in the sides of the arena.

'The work was carried out quickly and efficiently. Once a body had been drained, it was removed from its chain and carried back up the steps; immediately, another took its place. The females did not resist; most approached their death with bowed heads and resignation. A few cried out in fear at the approach of the knife; very occasionally, a shrill scream was to be heard echoing across the vastness of the stadium.

'For seven days the work went on, until gradually the arena was filled with blood, almost to shoulder height. From time to time, the mages stirred in small dilutions of other liquids so that it should not congeal. Finally this work of madness was accomplished. At the end of the seventh day, the last female had been killed, and our race now consisted of only males. The path had been cleared; the weakness excised; the stain washed clean. That is what they believed had been achieved.'

'I don't understand,' Grimalkin said. 'Which weakness do you speak of?'

'It was thought that females made us weak. That they softened males with their wiles and undermined the savagery that is necessary to be a warrior.'

'Do *you* believe that?' Grimalkin asked, staring into the eyes of Slither.

He shook his head. 'A warrior must always guard against a softening of his nature, but it can come from many sources. It was an act of madness to kill our females, though all societies can temporarily lapse into insanity.'

I felt sick, but was astonished to hear Grimalkin say, 'Yes, I think you are correct.'

'Of course, such events are hard to forecast, but in the case of my own people I'm sure that the madness will return. And I know the circumstances that will bring it about.'

'Have you seen this? Or is it common knowledge amongst your people?' Grimalkin demanded.

'It is a faith that our people blindly hold to. But we mages have probed the future and think that it is very likely to occur again.'

'When will that happen?'

'I know not the "when" but I know the "why",' Slither replied. 'When our god, Talkus, is born, Kobalos strength will be tripled, and we will surge out of Valkarky in a holy war that will wipe humankind from the face of this world. That is what my people believe. They will embrace the insanity of total war.'

'I thank you for being truthful,' Grimalkin said. 'The history of your people is terrible – it explains why you steal human women and practise slavery. I oppose such a thing with every fibre of my being; however, I will keep my word regarding your sale of Nessa. I will leave your city secretly, but will join you again soon. First I will escort you on your journey south to deliver the younger sister to her aunt and uncle. Finally I will accompany you as you travel towards the Dendar Mountains. I wish to see the kulad of Karpotha where human females are traded.'

Hearing her words, I could not prevent a sob from escaping

my lips. For a moment I had thought that Grimalkin might stand up to Slither and demand that I be given my freedom to go with Bryony. Now I saw that she would honour her promise to him – a beast amongst beasts! These animals had killed their own females, and now I was to be delivered into their filthy hands.

CHAPTER 22
THE KANGADON

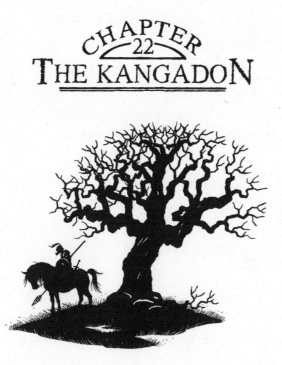

We left Valkarky on good mounts, shod in the Kobalos manner so that they could walk more easily through the snow. Our saddlebags contained grain to feed the horses and, additionally, sufficient oscher to meet any emergencies. We also had provisions of our own for the journey.

There was no sign of the witch. She had done as she'd said and left Valkarky secretly, riding on ahead.

The two purrai had stopped their sobbing at last, but they looked pale, their eyes downcast, evidently still in the grip of grief. I shook my head at their foolishness. What was done was done. There was no profit in dwelling on it. The minds of humans were indeed weak.

At the gate the High Mage, Balkai, the most senior of the Triumvirate, said a bitter farewell to me. A poor loser, he was scowling as we parted ways. I knew that he had no love for haizda mages; he was made uneasy by the fact that we worked alone, far from the city, and thus beyond his scrutiny and control.

'You ride away an apparent victor,' he said, leaning close and whispering into my right ear so that those in attendance could not hear. 'Your shakamure magic may have helped you to survive a little while longer, but your days are numbered.'

'I did not use my magic in the arena,' I replied truthfully. 'However, before I arrived here I used it quite legally in order to reclaim my purrai. It is my right. It is an expression of what I am!'

'We cannot forget what you have done – you haizdas must be taught a lesson. It is nothing personal – just an exercise of power to maintain our rule. Eblis, foremost of the Shaiksa, will come after you; he will be armed with the Kangadon, the Lance of Power.'

'The trial has exonerated me and allowed me to go free, with my purrai acknowledged as my own. In sending an assassin after me you act illegally!' I hissed defiantly.

'Listen well, fool,' Balkai continued, his mouth still close to my ear. 'We the Triumvirate always act in our own best interests. We make, shape and break the law when necessary. I wish you a safe journey until you die.'

I bowed and smiled sarcastically. 'I thank you for your kind solicitations, Lord. After I have killed Eblis, I will hang his ugly head from the tallest branch of my ghanbala tree. It is early spring in my haizda and the crows will be hungry. They consider eyeballs a great delicacy.'

Then, without another glance at him, I mounted my horse and rode with Nessa and Bryony away from Valkarky. I felt the eyes of the High Mage boring into my back. He was seething with anger and his discomfort made my heart sing.

In truth, I had hoped to ride away from the city bathed in goodwill, able to put the unpleasantness of my visit behind me. But some people cannot let things go, and Balkai seemed determined to have one last attempt to end my life.

Eblis was the leader and most formidable of the Shaiksa assassins. He was known as He Who Cannot Be Defeated. The order advanced their knowledge each time one of their brotherhood died in combat, his dying thoughts communicating the manner of that demise. Some of them would also have studied my fight in the arena; by now they would be well versed in my style of fighting and might have detected a weakness, unknown even to me, which they might exploit.

Using powerful magic, they had created a dangerous weapon, the Kangadon, also known as the Lance of Power or the Lance That Cannot Be Broken. Its other name is the King Slayer, for it had been used to kill the last King of Valkarky: his immense strength and formidable magical defences had proved inadequate against such a weapon. There were many rumours about this blade, but none other than a Shaiksa had ever set eyes upon it, let alone witnessed it in action.

There was nothing I could do but deal with the threat when it came, so I thrust the problem from my mind and led the sisters south. I would try to keep my promise and return the younger purra to her aunt and uncle. There was no point in telling the two girls about the new danger. If I died before parting ways with them, they would be returned to Valkarky – either to be eaten or to face a lifetime of slavery.

The wind was blowing from the south with a promise of spring, and on the fifth day we entered a forest of tall pines. Amongst them was a scattering of deciduous trees, their stark branches already softened with new green shoots.

As evening approached, we made camp and soon I had a fire going and was heating soup for the purrai, its aroma steaming up into the cold crisp air. They seemed subdued and deep in thought, so I left Nessa stirring the liquid, watched by the hungry Bryony, and decided to go hunting. My needs were different. I needed blood and raw meat.

The snow was thin on the ground, with tussocks of grass showing through. However, it was deep enough to show fresh tracks, and soon my belly was rumbling with hunger as I closed in on my prey. It had already gone to ground, but its shallow burrow offered no protection and I reached in and seized it by the tail. It was an anchiette, fully mature and about as long as my arm. Its blood was warm and sweet, and I drank my fill before picking the delicate meat from its skinny ribs. Finally I chewed, crunched and swallowed its tasty leg-bones.

My hunger somewhat assuaged, I turned to retrace my steps.

It was then that I noticed something carved into the trunk of a nearby tree.

It had been gouged into the bark quite recently, and I examined it closely, tracing its shape with my forefinger. It was the simple depiction of a pair of scissors. Why should anyone wish to carve such a thing here? I wondered. Was it a marker so that others might follow?

And then I remembered that the witch assassin had a pair of scissors in a leather sheath. Had *she* carved that symbol, and if so, why?

Grimalkin had said that she would escort us south and then on to the slave kulad, but this was the first sign that she might be somewhere close.

Again, I wondered if I could trust the witch. Why did she not reveal herself? Puzzled, I walked back to our camp.

The next day, after the purrai had eaten, I removed the over-shoes of the horses and we continued on our way south.

Two days later we came to a temperate valley. Sheltered from the northern winds, it had its own micro-climate. The deciduous trees now outnumbered the conifers, and their branches were already covered in fresh green leaves. The snow had melted here, making the ground squelchy, and in places our mounts churned it to soft mud.

The setting sun was bright, shining into our eyes out of a clear sky. Birds sang overhead, insects droned, and we rode along slowly, looking for a place to camp.

Suddenly everything became unnaturally quiet.

The birds ceased their spring songs. Even the insects fell silent. All that could be heard was the breathing of the horses and the slow rhythm of hooves on the soft ground.

Then I understood the reason why.

Directly ahead was a large solitary oak tree. It was gnarled, black and twisted, all life driven from it by the cold of the winter. Beneath that tree the Shaiksa waited. He was sitting astride a black stallion; a long lance, which he gripped with a black leather gauntlet, was angled back to rest easily against his shoulder. He was clad in black armour of the highest quality; plate lay across plate, sure to turn aside the strongest blade. He also wore a helmet with a lowered visor so that only the throat was truly vulnerable. Balkai had been true to his word: here was the assassin he had promised to send against me.

I could not see his eyes. It always bothers me when I cannot gaze into the eyes of an enemy. I feel at a disadvantage.

The neck of the assassin was adorned with a triple necklace of skulls; some, though incredibly small, were human. The Shaiksa used magic to shrink the skulls of their defeated enemies; thus they were able to decorate themselves with many such signs of victory without impeding their movements. The number of such adornments told me that I was indeed gazing upon Eblis, the most deadly of all the Shaiksa Brotherhood. The lance he held was the Kangadon, which he had used to kill the last King of Valkarky nine centuries earlier.

I heard the sound of hooves behind me as the sisters wisely moved their mounts out of the way of the expected attack.

Taking the initiative, I drew two blades and charged towards Eblis, my mount gathering speed as it pounded over the muddy ground. So sudden was my assault that the Shaiksa didn't have time to bring up the lance properly. I was upon him before he could target me.

My blades flashed in the sunlight and there was the clash of metal on metal. The one in my right hand found the join between two armoured plates on Eblis's chest. I thrust it upwards into the gap and it jammed. Whether it had penetrated the flesh was impossible to say. But the blade in my left hand shattered against the Shaiksa's armour and I tossed away the hilt of the broken weapon. As I turned my mount, ready to attack again, I drew the sabre.

But this time I lacked the advantage of surprise. Eblis was ready for my attack and he urged his own horse forward too, the sharp tip of the Kangadon aimed straight at my heart. I twisted in my saddle, ensuring that the point of the lance missed me, but I had no opportunity to strike a blow of my own.

We brought our horses round and thundered towards each other again, the assassin once more lowering the lance into a horizontal position, his horse kicking up a spray of mud behind him.

However, I focused my concentration, and now I created a magical shield identical to the one that had thwarted the hyb's sharp talons. It was small and bright, gleaming in the air, no bigger than a hand's span, but I positioned it precisely with my mind and held it firm so that the lance, despite its magical properties, might be deflected.

But at the moment of contact I suddenly understood how Eblis had defeated the King of Valkarky so long ago. The king would no doubt have used a magical shield even more powerful than my own, but at the moment of his death he must have recognized the true power of the Kangadon: nothing could deflect it from its target.

And so it was now. The tip of the lance went through my shield like a knife through butter and sought out my heart. I was a fraction of a second away from death. Only one thing remained for me to do; I could not deflect the Kangadon, so I had to evade it.

I twisted in the saddle, avoiding its tip by the thickness of a butterfly's wing, and threw myself off my horse. I absorbed some of the impact by tucking my arms and legs in close to my body and rolling forward as I met the ground. It was soft after the melting of the winter's snow and that helped to cushion the blow, but nevertheless, the air was punched from my lungs. The sabre flew out of my hand and I lay sprawled on the ground while my deadly opponent quickly turned his horse and charged at me again.

I managed to sit up, but I was befuddled, struggling to clear my head after my heavy tumble. Eblis had almost reached me, the tip of the Kangadon still aimed unerringly at my heart. I thought my end had come, when suddenly I heard the drumming of other hooves and something rushed towards him from my left.

It was a white horse and rider. Now they were between me and the assassin, and they met the force of his charge. The white horse whinnied and toppled over, throwing its rider into the air like a rag doll. I glimpsed her face as she spun over and over before hitting the ground hard.

It was little Nessa. She had tried to save me and had now paid the price.

Her mount whinnied again, and rolled over before heaving itself upright. I glanced towards Nessa. She was lying face down and was not moving. Her death had been quick and kind – far better than the one she would have faced at the hands of the Shaiksa once I had been dispatched. She was the luckiest of the three sisters. The tawny death was quick, but it was extremely painful to undergo, with hot bubbles popping inside your stomach and intestines, and your flesh melting from within.

I realized I had failed to keep my promise to Old Rowler. Once I was dead, the youngest child would be slain too, her throat cut by this assassin. She would suffer the same death they had originally intended for her back in the tower. I had merely delayed the inevitable. I felt angry and bitter at the prospect of my defeat. It had all been for nothing.

Eblis brought his horse round in a slow arc, his lance at the ready. My head was clearing now and I looked around for my sabre. I was unable to deflect the blade, but at least I could die with a weapon in my hand. But my legs simply refused to work: all I could do was struggle up onto my knees.

The Shaiksa raised his visor and smiled at me. He wished me to gaze upon the face of the one who would slay me. I did not waste any words and kept my expression impassive. Inside, I was seething with anger at the thought that Balkai would get his way. I had proved myself in the trial; in sending this assassin, he had showed no honour. He was unscrupulous and corrupt.

Although I knew that I would die here, I wanted to reach my sabre: I would do my best to hurt Eblis so that he would always remember our encounter. One had to die sometime, and to fall to the greatest of the Shaiksa assassins – He Who Cannot Be Defeated – was a worthy death.

He charged again. I twisted away, but the tip of the lance pierced my right shoulder and Eblis jerked it upwards violently, lifting me off my feet. For a moment I was helpless and in terrible pain, but my weight, in addition to the length of the lance, meant that he could not hold me aloft for more than a few seconds. The moment he was forced to lower it, I slid down the lance, hit the ground and rolled to the side.

When I got to my knees again, blood was running down my arm and dripping into the mud. In moments I would surely be dead, but still I would not give up, and I began to crawl across the mud towards my sabre. It seemed a long way away; at any moment Eblis might charge again and transfix me with his lance – maybe this time through the heart.

As I made my way painfully along, I kept my eyes on him. He was staring at me but did not urge his mount forward.

Everything was very still and quiet. Then I realized that he was not looking at me after all. I risked a quick backward glance.

Behind me, slightly to my left, I saw another rider on a stallion as black and powerful as Eblis's. I knew that rider. It was a purra.

It was Grimalkin, the human witch assassin.

CHAPTER
23
HE WHO CAN NEVER DIE

Grimalkin was holding the necklace of bones that she wore around her neck. Hers must be bones from the hands of her defeated enemies rather than the shrunken skulls worn by Eblis. She was tapping and stroking them in some mysterious ritualistic fashion. As I watched, she released the bones and drew a long dagger from one of her scabbards, then approached me, her horse stepping delicately across the soft mud.

'Get up off your knees, Slither,' she commanded. 'Kill your enemy with this. Kill him before he kills you. Never give in! Never surrender!'

She threw the dagger towards me. It spun over and over

through the air, but I reached up with a cry of pain and caught it by the hilt.

There was something odd about that weapon. The moment I lifted my tail it told me that the blade was crafted from a silver alloy. My eyes told me something even more astounding.

The hilt was crafted in the shape of a skelt's head, and its eyes were two rubies. It was the image of our unborn god, Talkus. As I watched, the ruby eyes shed tears of blood that dripped onto the mud close to my feet to mingle with my own. It was without doubt a blade of power. I could feel the magical force emanating from it.

Grimalkin smiled and backed her horse away from me. Filled with new hope and strength, I got to my feet. Eblis had been gazing warily at Grimalkin, but now, as she moved away, his attention came back to me – his target.

He charged straight towards me. I took a deep breath and stood my ground, bringing the whole of my concentration to bear upon the task at hand. As the tip of the lance came within range I stepped to one side to avoid being trampled by the stallion, lifted the blade and parried the tip of the spear.

To my astonishment, the blade did not break. It deflected the lance and scraped along its whole length, sending up a shower of sparks. When it reached the Shaiksa's gauntlets and found his hands, he cried out in shock. He released the Kangadon, and it spun upwards out of his grasp, turning over and over in the air.

Then, in a moment of *whalakai* – the perception that comes to a haizda mage but rarely – I was aware of every nuance of the situation in a flash of insight.

I knew what I must do! I sliced sideways, my arm moving almost too fast to be seen, and struck the spinning lance with my blade.

The Kangadon split into two pieces.

Thus the Lance That Cannot Be Broken was no more.

But it was not for nothing that Eblis had survived and prevailed as an assassin for over two thousand years. The lance was destroyed and he was wounded, but he summoned his strength and attacked once more. This time he wielded two more long blades as he attempted to ride me down.

Once again I struck out with the skelt blade, and then spun away quickly to avoid being trampled. His horse galloped onwards, nostrils snorting steam into the chill air. But Eblis fell, hit the ground hard, and lay there without moving.

I approached and looked down at my enemy – but, to my own surprise, I did not deal the final blow. It was not a conscious decision. Something within me had chosen another way for this to end. I waited in silence, still gripping the blade. After many minutes Eblis rolled onto his stomach and struggled to his feet. His hands were empty of weapons. He had lost them in the fall. Nevertheless I waited patiently while he retrieved them from the mud, which had been churned up by the galloping hooves.

Then we began to fight at close quarters. We were evenly matched and the struggle continued for a long time. Soon the sun went down and the light began to fail. Now we were fighting in darkness and I used my shakamure magic to see my enemy. I also drew upon my other magical reserves to bolster my strength. No doubt Eblis employed his own magic, because his blades were guided with great accuracy, and for a while I was hard pressed just to parry them. We fought in silence – all that could be heard was grunts, the clash of blades and our boots churning the mud.

But slowly I began to gain the ascendancy, and at last I brought my enemy to his knees and lifted the dagger for the killing blow.

As I did so, I felt a hand staying my arm.

'You have won, Slither, but now he is mine,' whispered the voice of Grimalkin in my ear. 'Return the blade to my hand.'

What could I do but acquiesce? After all, I had won a great victory and I owed the witch for that. Without her intervention I would have died in the mud. So I returned the blade to her and walked across to the place where Nessa lay.

I knelt down beside her. She was still breathing, just, but her life-signs were slowly fading. I had a little magic remaining to me, so I placed my hand on her forehead and let it seep into her body until she began to revive.

After a while I helped her up into a sitting position and she opened her eyes.

'You were dying, little Nessa, but I have revived you with my strength. It is no more than what I owe you.'

Just as she had saved me when bitten by the snake, now I had repaid her. She stared at me for a while and seemed about to make some reply, but then I heard a sound from behind that made the hairs stand up on the back of my neck.

Shaiksa assassins do not scream. And yet Eblis, the bravest, strongest and most ruthless of them all, cried out. His screams went on for a very long time.

Nessa looked at me, her eyes widening at the sound. I found the sounds pleasing – but obviously she did not. The assassin was being killed slowly, and his dying thoughts were being sent out to the rest of his brotherhood. Even as he died, their knowledge was being advanced. But what were they learning?

In another moment of whalakai, I understood what was happening. They were not only learning – they were being taught. That lesson was being given by Grimalkin: just as she had carved the symbol of her scissors on trees to mark her territory and warn off her enemies, so, now, she was sending the whole Shaiksa Brotherhood a message.

She was telling them who she was; what she was capable of; teaching them all about pain and fear.

And then, in a loud voice, she called out her verbal message to the brotherhood: 'Keep away from me,' she warned, 'or what I did to your brother, so I will do to you! Those who pursue me will die a death such as this! I am Grimalkin.'

So it was that the Lance That Cannot Be Broken was indeed broken, and He Who Cannot Be Defeated was slain and left this world after over two thousand years as an undefeated Shaiksa assassin.

And in that moment I knew that the witch assassin was the most deadly warrior I had ever encountered. So now a great challenge lay ahead. One day I must fight and defeat her. To accomplish that would be the summit of my endeavours as a haizda mage.

When later I examined the body of Eblis to see what had been done to him, I could see nothing that could have made him shriek so musically. It is true that she had carved the symbol of her scissors on his forehead, but there was nothing else. I had to admit that there were many things I could learn from the human witch.

CHAPTER 24
DAUGHTER OF DARKNESS

Nessa was bruised and battered, but because of my help had survived her fall; her greatest hurt was still the loss of her sister, Susan.

Later, after the two girls had cried themselves to sleep, the witch and I talked by the campfire.

'The magnificent blade that I used to defeat Eblis – where did you obtain it?' I asked.

'It does not belong to me,' she replied. 'I hold it in trust for another and must return it to him.'

'May I see it again?' I asked.

The witch smiled grimly, showing her pointed teeth, and for a moment I thought that she might refuse me. Then she drew it out of its scabbard and handed it to me. I held it carefully, turning it over and over in my hands. I sensed its power immediately.

'This is a very special blade. Who made it?' I asked.

'It was crafted by one of our gods, little mage. We have our own god of blacksmiths and he is called Hephaestus.'

'It is strange that he should choose a skelt's head for the hilt,' I observed. 'Talkus, our God Who Is Yet to Be, will assume this likeness at the moment of his birth.'

'I remember what you said,' the witch said with a frown. 'Your people will begin a holy war and try to drive us into the sea.'

'Then we will rule the whole world,' I told her.

'It will certainly be an interesting time!' she said. 'Were you to attempt such a thing, my people would certainly offer fierce resistance. And then we would eventually pull down the walls of Valkarky and rid the world of the Kobalos. So let us hope that it is a long time before Talkus enters this world!'

I handed the blade back to her without comment, but then several thoughts came to me almost simultaneously.

'The star-stone – is it valuable to humans?' I asked. 'Is that why you entered our territory and approached Valkarky? It seems an odd coincidence that you should be nearby when it fell.'

'It was not a coincidence. I knew when and where it would fall,' the witch retorted.

'Did you use magic to learn that?'

211

'We witches can sometimes scry the future; we are also able to "long-sniff" approaching danger. But I will admit that it was actually a strange dream that revealed the coming of the stone to me – one that seemed so real I thought I had awakened. There was a blinding light so fierce that I feared my eyes would be burned from my head. Then a voice told me where and when it would fall – and then, once it was in my possession, what I must do with it.'

'Did the voice that came out of the light also warn you of the danger from my people?'

'I already knew that the piece of ore would plummet to earth near to your city,' she replied. 'It fell exactly as predicted, but then, while I waited for it to cool so that I could carry it away south, I sniffed the approach of your warriors. I fought them, but they were too numerous.'

'Now that it is once more in your possession, what will you do with it?'

'This is a blade from the dark and not truly suitable for the one who must wield it!' she exclaimed, holding the skelt-shaped hilt out towards me. 'So I will forge a new blade – one even greater and more potent!'

'Who is the one it is destined for? Is he a king?'

'At this time he is the apprentice of a spook – one skilled in dealing with the dark and its servants. He is the only one who has the ability to destroy the Fiend for ever. This dark blade is one of three that he must use to achieve that end. But if he survives, he may have other tasks awaiting him.'

'What other tasks?'

'I have scryed the future and know that further challenges await him – but all is uncertain. Scrying is an imperfect art. He may even die in his attempt to kill the Fiend. I looked into a mirror, striving to see his future, but it became cloudy with doubt. I will forge the blade for him, anyway.'

'You hope to forge a better blade than that created by your blacksmith god?' I said, shaking my head at her presumption. 'My people call such vaunted ambition hubris. Pride is the greatest sin of all – one that can call down the combined anger of the gods.'

'Nevertheless I am determined to try,' she replied. 'This is what the voice commanded: I must forge a blade of light. It shall be called the Star Blade.'

'You belong to what you call the "dark", and yet you would create its antithesis. It is strange indeed that a daughter of darkness should forge a blade of light!' I commented.

'We live in strange times,' the witch replied. 'It is also strange that I, a witch, should have formed an alliance with the enemies of my clan. But this is what has forced the situation upon us,' she said, lifting the leather sack that contained the head of their dark god. 'The Fiend must be destroyed. Nothing else matters but that.'

CHAPTER
25
FAREWELL TO MY SISTER

❧NESSA❧

We continued south, heading for the village of
Stoneleigh on the edge of Pwodente. I shared a horse
with Bryony. It broke my heart to think that though we were
now so close, and I could put my arms around her, it would be
for the last time.

I leaned forward and put my mouth next to her ear. 'Try to
keep hope alive in your heart, Bryony,' I whispered. 'One day I
will find a way to return to you, I swear it!'

'I'm sure you'll find a way, Nessa!' she exclaimed with a
smile. 'You're so clever, I'm certain it won't take you long.'

Despite my sister's youthful optimism I knew that it was

214

extremely unlikely that we would ever meet again. But at least Bryony had the prospect of a long and happy life. I could still hardly believe that Susan had been taken from us. The witch had fought alongside the beast, and somehow they had prevailed – but at what a terrible cost! Poor Susan must have been so frightened – and to die such a death! The pain in my heart was unbearable.

If only my life could have been taken instead, I would have willingly given it so that she might live.

'What if my aunt and uncle are cruel to me?' Bryony said suddenly.

'They're family. They will be good to you, I feel certain of that,' I said softly.

In truth, I was certain of nothing. Times were hard, and if our aunt and uncle were scratching a living here on the edge of Kobalos territory, the last thing they needed was another hungry mouth to feed.

That night around the campfire, we discussed how Bryony might best be handed over to our relatives.

'If we show our face, it will cause great alarm,' Grimalkin told the beast, 'for you are Kobalos and I am clearly a witch. As a result we will be hunted down and thus be forced to kill our pursuers. The girls' relatives might even be among them.'

This was indeed the likely outcome of being seen, and I nodded in agreement.

'I suggest we cloak ourselves,' Grimalkin continued.

'That may not be necessary. Let us see the lie of the land.

We may be able to send the youngest purra out alone and watch from afar,' Slither proposed.

'Yes, but we must be certain that she is well-received and accepted into the family,' I insisted. 'After all, we have never met them. They may not wish to be burdened with my sister. They may even be dead by now, and there is no guarantee that a small community struggling to survive would welcome even one extra mouth to feed. I need some reassurance that my sister is safe.'

The following morning we completed the final stage of the journey to the dwelling place of our aunt and uncle.

Keeping to the left bank, we followed the river downstream and approached the last bridge before the Western Sea, which we could now see in the distance. There was a small wood between us and the bridge. It couldn't have been better for what we planned.

'This is perfect,' said Grimalkin. 'We can wait hidden within the trees at the edge of the wood and yet watch Bryony cross the bridge.'

'But if our aunt and uncle take you in, you must come back to the bridge and wave to show us that all is well,' I said. 'Promise me that.'

'I promise,' Bryony said, her voice choked with emotion. 'They'll ask me about you and Susan,' she continued, her eyes brimming with tears. 'What shall I say?'

I thought hard. As far as I knew, Father had never exchanged letters with his kin in Pwodente. They might not even know of his daughters, or that his wife was dead. But it was better to approximate the truth as far as possible.

'You must be brave, Bryony,' I replied. 'Tell them how our father died, but say that your sisters stayed behind to try and work the farm with a view to selling it eventually. Say things were hard and they felt unable to care for you properly and hoped that one day they might join you or maybe send for you to return. Say that you have been accompanied by travellers who have gone many miles out of their way to bring you safely here and they cannot afford to tarry longer but just wish to know that all is well. Could you say that?'

'I'll do my best, Nessa. I'll try.' She was being as brave as she could.

So we dismounted and waited just within the trees. Bryony and I withdrew a little distance from Grimalkin and Slither and exchanged a tearful farewell – one of such duration that the beast began to pace up and down in a most agitated fashion, his tail up high, and I knew that we were testing his patience to its limits.

But at last, after a final hug, Bryony gulped and then set off towards the river. I watched her go, trying to hold back the tears. I knew what it cost her to leave me behind and I was proud of her courage. Her figure grew smaller and smaller as she approached the bridge and crossed it to disappear amongst the small huddle of cottages that we judged to be Stoneleigh.

We waited in silence, Slither displaying increasing impatience, and after about an hour, three people came over the bridge and looked at us across the meadow. I saw a man and a woman, and between them stood my sister, Bryony. She raised her hand and waved three times.

That was the prearranged signal that she was well and had found sanctuary with our aunt and uncle. With that final wave I was satisfied: we were free to head northwest towards the dreaded slave market. Bryony's new life was just beginning; mine was as good as over. I did not expect to live long as a slave of the Kobalos.

CHAPTER 26
THE SLAVE KULAD

As we rode, my spirits were high, knowing that once Nessa was sold I would be free to return to my haizda. I was looking forward to going home. But Nessa countered my happy, optimistic mood with a constant flow of tears which I somehow found disturbing. The threat of skaiium was still there. Although I tried my utmost, I found it hard to rid myself of the memory of some of her actions.

She had given me her blood to revive me after I'd been bitten by the skulka; much later, she had ridden between me and Eblis, thus giving me a chance of life. These actions could, I suppose, be accounted for in the same way as her request for a knife in order to help fight the Haggenbrood:

she had simply been trying to ensure the survival of her sisters.

But I could not forget how she had pressed her forehead against mine – such a daring thing for a purra to do. Again, it was prompted by a desire to persuade me to save Bryony, and had resulted in my slaying of the Nunc and then the Shaiksa assassin. But I could not forget the touch of her skin on mine.

A small part of me wanted to set her free to go and live with her sister, but I could not countenance that. I was a haizda mage; I had to be strong and fight any hint of weakness within myself. In any case, it was important that I sell a slave and meet the requirements of Bindos; otherwise I would find myself an outlaw once more.

We headed north, crossed the Fittzanda Fissure without mishap, experiencing just a few mild tremors, and soon we were travelling through snow once more. It lay thin on the ground now, with a crisp crust of ice; the skies were clear. Even in the land of the Kobalos there was a short summer, and now it was on its way.

We began to climb into the foothills of the Dendar Mountains, and just before dusk on the second day, we saw Karpotha, the largest of all the slave kulads, in the distance. It was a broad, dark tower rising up into the sky; a large walled courtyard surrounded it. This was where the holding pens for the purrai were located.

I wished to be done with the business of selling Nessa. All I wanted to do now was to return to my haizda and replenish my magic. It was seriously depleted – I didn't like to admit it, but that was why I had rejected the idea of cloaking myself in order to hide from the child's family. I scarcely had the magical strength to do so, and I might yet have need of my last reserves.

We made camp under an outcrop of rock and I told the witch that, soon after dawn, I would take Nessa to the kulad and sell her.

Grimalkin made no reply and was silent for a long time. Around the campfire the atmosphere was cooler than the northerly breeze, and all three of us ate in silence. Finally, without a word, Nessa wrapped herself in her blanket and withdrew from us under the shelter of the cliff. Once the purra had gone, the witch started to talk.

'Where did you get that coat?' she asked. 'I've never seen one like it.'

'It's a sign of office,' I replied. 'Once each haizda mage completes his noviciate, he is given such a coat. There are thirteen buttons symbolizing the thirteen truths.'

'The thirteen truths? What are they?'

'If you knew that, then you too would be a haizda mage,' I told her. 'Perhaps one day I could teach you. But it would take thirty years of your life or more. Such knowledge is not truly suited to short-lived humans.'

She smiled grimly. 'I have not thirty years to spare just now, but one day I may visit you again. Maybe then you *could* teach me a little of your craft. My sister witches in Pendle are conservative and keep to the old ways, but I like to learn from other cultures and disciplines and increase my knowledge in new methods.

'But now I will speak to you of a matter that concerns me much. I ask again that you do not sell the girl in the slave market. She has been brave, and by some of her actions has ensured your own survival. But for the danger to the two girls, I would not have loaned you the dagger that you used to defeat the assassin.'

'What you say is true,' I admitted, 'but I must refuse your request. Have I not explained my situation to you already? Do you forget so quickly? It is not that I need the money, but according to a Kobalos law called Bindos, every forty years each citizen must sell at least one purra in the slave markets. That sale is carefully recorded. Otherwise we forgo our citizenship and are cast out of Valkarky, never to be welcomed there again. Consequently, we become outlaws and may be killed on sight.'

'So by law you are forced to become a party to the slave trade that is at the very heart of your society. It is a clever piece of legislation, designed to bind you together with your common values.'

'That is true,' I replied. 'Without the trade we could not breed and survive. We would become extinct.'

'Are there no dissenters?'

I nodded. 'There is a group within the city that call themselves the *Skapien*. Some say they have no central organization but work within small independent isolated cells. What they achieve or attempt nobody knows. Occasionally one declares himself publicly; after a brief trial, he is executed as a traitor whose aim is to destroy the state.'

'Do you personally know anybody who has been executed in this way?'

'No,' I replied. 'I visit the city only rarely, and apart from the haizda servants like Hom, who bring me news, I have no friends or acquaintances.'

'What about other haizda mages – do you communicate with them?'

'Only if we meet by chance,' I told the witch.

'Then yours is a lonely life indeed.'

'It is what I choose,' I replied. 'I wish for no other. Now I must ask *you* a question . . . You promised not to hinder me. Will you keep your word?'

'Yes, I will keep my word,' the witch replied. 'You may enter the kulad tomorrow and sell a slave – which means that you will have met your obligation as a citizen. But after that our trade is over. Do you understand?'

'You mean that from then on we are enemies?'

'Perhaps we will be somewhere between allies and enemies. But for now we will go our separate ways.'

Soon after that we retired for the night, but later I awoke to the murmur of voices. The witch and Nessa were whispering together. I attempted to tune in my hearing and listen to their conversation, but they immediately fell silent. It seemed to me that they had been plotting something – though I was not unduly concerned. Whatever else she was, I believed the human witch to be honourable – one who would keep her word. Tomorrow, without hindrance, I would sell Nessa, and thus fulfil my duties as a citizen for another four decades.

For the remainder of the night I slept well. At some point, however, I began to dream, and it was one of the strangest that I have ever experienced. In it I rescued Nessa from some deadly threat. It seemed so real. Afterwards, I remembered all but the very end; it was a most enjoyable dream – and whatever occurred at the end, it was extremely pleasurable.

I awoke at dawn to find that the witch had already left our camp. No doubt she did not wish to see one of her race being sold into slavery. But at least she had kept her word not to hinder me. So, wasting no time on breakfasting, Nessa and I mounted our horses in silence, and I led her towards the kulad.

She looked sad, so as we rode I offered her a few kind words of advice, which I hoped might be useful to her in her new life as a slave.

'Once you have left my possession, little Nessa, be subservient and deferential at all times. Never look your new masters in the eye. That is most important. And when they begin the auction, stand tall on the platform, with your head held high but your gaze always on the boards at your feet. Thank them for each stroke of the whip upon your skin and each cut of the blade into your flesh. That is expected. By such means, not only will you command a higher price and please all who gaze upon you; it will be the means to live as long a life as can reasonably be expected for a purra.'

'How long *do* slaves live?' Nessa asked.

'Once they reach adulthood, some purrai live as long as ten or twelve years, but once their flesh is no longer young and the taste of their blood becomes less sweet, they are slain and their ageing bodies consumed by the whoskor, the multi-legged builders of Valkarky.'

'Then I don't have much to look forward to,' she observed sadly. 'It can't be right to treat people in this manner.'

I did not reply, for now I saw the dark stone of the outer kulad wall looming over us; it was time to get down to business. From the northeast, the hooves of horses and the feet of manacled slaves had churned the route to the fortress into a dirty river of mud and slush. I presented myself at the gate, declared my purpose, and gained entry. Once that was done I did not linger, forcing the girl onwards. The truth was, I was still feeling slightly uncomfortable at the idea of disposing of Nessa in this way, and I wished to get it over with as quickly as possible.

Despite the early hour, there was a bustle of activity within the open courtyard of the kulad. Purrai were already being brought in chains to the three wooden bidding platforms where large groups of Kobalos merchants were gathered. At least a dozen armed Oussa guards were present. They looked surly, and clearly considered watching over the proceedings here to be beneath them. No doubt they thought they would be better employed hunting down the witch – it was rumoured that she had fled south. They would still be smarting from the shame of seeing four of their number dispatched by her when she was first captured.

I noticed that some gave me glances of recognition that verged on respect. No doubt they had witnessed my defeat of the Haggenbrood.

I dismounted, pulled Nessa unceremoniously down off her horse and dragged her over to the nearest platform. I would have liked to be gentler, but in so public a gathering I had no choice but to conform to the norms of this society. It took less than a minute to complete the transaction with the merchant.

'I offer one hundred valcrons for the purra,' he said, rubbing his hands together.

A valcron is the daily wage of a lowly Kobalos foot soldier, and I knew that he would make at least twice that amount when he put her up for auction. However, I was in no mood to haggle and simply wished to seal the transaction as quickly as possible. Money did not concern me; I simply had to meet my legal obligations. So I nodded, accepting the offer, and he counted the small coins into a bag.

'What do you offer for this horse?' I asked, indicating the mare that Nessa had been riding.

'Two hundred and twenty valcrons,' he said with a smile, and began rubbing his hands together again in the irritating manner merchants deem appropriate when conducting business.

He added the coins to the bag, handed it over, and the deal was done.

Thus I got more for the animal than I had for Nessa. It was because she was so skinny. Such purrai never attract high prices.

However, the important thing was that the transaction was recorded against my name, and would now be entered into the Bindos records. I had discharged my duties as a citizen.

The servants of the merchant dragged Nessa over to face him, and I was glad to see that she was following my advice, keeping her eyes respectfully upon the ground rather than meeting his eyes. It had always disconcerted me when she met my own gaze so levelly. A trained purra must never do that. She must accept her new station or suffer terribly.

The merchant drew the knife from his belt and swiftly made two cuts to Nessa's forearm. She did not even flinch. Then I distinctly heard her say, 'Thank you, Master.'

Something inside me rebelled against this. For all that Nessa had been my property, I had never cut her.

But there was nothing I could do about it. I rode away, resisting the urge to glance back at her as I approached the gate. I knew that I had to fight the onset of skaiium with every last bit of my strength. It was difficult, but I was strong and did not yield.

CHAPTER 27
A CRY IN THE NIGHT

Once through the gateway, I looked up at the sky and frowned. Clouds were racing in from the north. Such storms were rare in early spring, but they could strike with a terrible fury.

I could have returned to the kulad and sat it out there, but something inside me was reluctant to witness Nessa's new situation. However, it would soon be impossible to travel further, so I urged my horse back to the shelter of the cliff where we had spent the previous night.

By now the wind was rising, and no sooner had I retreated under the overhang than the first large flakes of snow began to whirl down from a sky the colour of lead.

Within minutes a blizzard was blowing out of the north.

As was usually the case with such early spring storms, it was, although fierce, of relatively short duration. After about six hours it began to abate, and by dusk the sky was clear. The approach of darkness caused me to delay my journey until first light: even though I was accustomed to travelling during the hours of darkness, there would be deep drifts in the foothills, making the going treacherous.

So, after feeding my horse, I settled down for the night. With no crisis looming and the delightful prospect of returning to my haizda, my mind was very calm, clear and sharp, and I began to review the events of recent weeks and re-evaluate my own role in what had taken place.

It seemed to me that I had behaved with honour and courage, and had fully discharged my obligation to Old Rowler. It was not my fault that Susan had died. I had done my best to save her. Alone, I had triumphed over a High Mage, a Shaiksa assassin and a dangerous hyb warrior. It was true that I had later worked in partnership with a human witch, but that had been necessary because of the great odds against me. Together with Grimalkin I had defeated the Haggenbrood, a wondrous achievement. Then, using the borrowed skelt blade, I had brought the mighty Eblis to his knees. How was it then that I had feared an attack of skaiium? Now, with a tranquil mind, I saw that such a thought was absurd. As a warrior mage, I had achieved near perfection.

Thus, safe from skaiium, I could afford to be generous. I

229

considered little Nessa again, and recognized that she had aided me at every turn. It was true that she had done so in order to ensure her sisters' survival, but her help had been timely and decisive. Suddenly I saw how I might repay her.

It was not possible to buy her back directly from the merchant with whom I had traded. Such a thing was forbidden. Even if, for a bribe, he agreed to the deal, my original sale would be considered void and I would no longer have fulfilled my duty. But there was another way.

Once Nessa had been sold on, I could buy her from her new owner without repercussions. No doubt it would cost me at least double what I had received for her, but money was not really a consideration for me. I could always get what I needed from my haizda. It would not even put me to much trouble. Because of the storm, her new owner would not yet have left Karpotha.

I resolved to go down to the kulad at first light and re-purchase Nessa. Then I would take her south to join her sister. Of course, I would sample a little of her blood on the way. Not enough to do her any real harm. She could hardly object to that, could she?

I awoke about an hour before dawn with a vague impression that I had just heard an animal cry out in the night. I heightened my senses and listened.

Within moments it came again – there was indeed a high, thin cry. But it was not an animal. It had come from either a human or a Kobalos throat. I lifted my tail, but unfortunately the wind from the north was still brisk and carried any scent away from me.

Soon there were other cries and screams, but I yawned and took little notice. No doubt a number of the purrai were being punished, probably those who had failed to attract a buyer. It served them right for not behaving in the correct manner. In retaliation, their owners would be whipping them or slicing into their flesh with sharp knives in places that would be concealed by their clothes.

At dawn I mounted my horse and set off directly for Karpotha. I needed to reach the kulad before Nessa's new owner left.

As soon as I crested the hill and looked down towards it, I knew that something was wrong. The gates were wide open.

I urged my horse forward across the fresh snow. It was then that I saw the tracks of many feet heading south, the snow churned up and no longer a pristine white. It seemed as if a large party of slaves had travelled in that direction. But why should that be? It made no sense at all. They should have been either going east or west towards the other slave markets, or northeast towards Valkarky itself – anywhere but south.

Then I noticed the first of the bodies. It was one of the small party of Oussa, who had escorted slaves to Karpotha. The warrior was lying face down. Beneath his head and upper body the snow had been turned to slush and stained bright red with his blood: his throat had been cut.

There were two more dead Oussa guards near the gates, and then I saw bloodied footprints heading away from the city – mostly northwards. Horses had gone in the same direction too.

What had happened? Why had they fled?

Inside the kulad there were bodies everywhere – Kobalos merchants as well as Oussa guards. The wooden platforms were slick with blood. Nothing lived. Nothing moved.

But there was no sign of the slaves – where could they be?

Then, for the first time, I noticed the shape carved into the gatepost:

This was the sign of the scissors that the witch assassin carried in a leather sheath. How could it possibly be marked here on the post? Had she returned?

No! She had not returned. She had been here all the time.

In a flash of understanding, I realized what had happened.

I had not sold Nessa at the slave market.

I had sold Grimalkin!

CHAPTER 28
WE WILL MEET AGAIN

What a fool I had been to trust the human witch!

Nessa had ridden away from the camp before I awoke, and Grimalkin, in a perfect simulacrum of the girl, had taken her place, just as she had in the arena. After slaughtering many of the Oussa and merchants, the witch had then led the slaves south towards the lands of the humans and freedom.

But she still had me to deal with.

She had broken her promise not to hinder me, and now I must pursue her and bring her to account.

It took me less than an hour to catch up with the witch and the escaped purrai.

She was riding at the head of the column of slaves, and there was another rider alongside her – surely it was Nessa. The hundred or so following them, walking two by two, carried sacks of provisions; they were dressed in sensible purrai clothes and were well-protected against the elements.

I began to charge towards the witch, passing along the left flank of the column, when, to my astonishment, the purrai broke formation and came between me and my enemy. Then, whooping and cheering, they began to hurl balls of snow in my direction, making my horse rear up in panic. It was astounding and unprecedented behaviour from purrai, and my mount, hardened by magic to face even the charge of a Shaiksa assassin, could not withstand the pelting of cold wet snow.

I was forced to retreat in order to bring the animal back under control. By the time I had done so, Grimalkin was already charging towards me, two blades held aloft, glittering with reflected light from the morning sun. But I had time to draw my sabre and urge my own mount forward so we came together hard and fast.

Neither of us managed to inflict any damage upon the other, and we came about quickly and began our second charge. The witch passed very close by on my left, and thrust at me viciously with a blade. However, using the last of my reserves of shakamure magic, I had already formed a magical shield and, positioning it perfectly, deflected her weapon, lunging towards her head as I did so.

She leaned away and I missed my target, but the tip of my sabre cut her shoulder, drawing blood. At that my heart sang with joy. Next time we passed I would finish her!

But as I faced my enemy again, I saw that now she wielded only one knife. Her other blade hadn't shattered against my shield, so why had she put it away? Perhaps the wound I had inflicted upon her left shoulder meant that she could no longer hold a blade with that hand? No, she now held this one in her left hand.

Then I concentrated my vision and noted that in her right hand she now carried the skelt sword – the weapon that had broken the Kangadon. It would do the same to my shield. Nor was I comfortable fighting against a blade with a hilt fashioned in the image of Talkus; he who, once born into this world, would be the most powerful of all Kobalos gods.

It was ominous. Did it signify my death? I wondered.

It did no good to think upon such things now; so, gathering my resolve, I spurred my horse forward once more. Closer and closer we approached, the hooves of our mounts sending a fine spray of snow up into the air. Blood was running down Grimalkin's left shoulder, but she was smiling.

My sabre would cut the smile from her face! I thought.

Then another horse was between us, forcing me to change direction, veering away to the left. It was Nessa. She galloped after me and we came to a halt some distance away.

I glanced back and saw that the witch had reined in her horse and was staring at us.

'You fool!' Nessa cried. 'Stop this at once or she will kill you. You don't have to die here. Return to your haizda and let us go on our way in peace.'

I was outraged by her words. She had called me a 'fool'! Who was she to speak to me in this manner? But before I could vent my anger, Grimalkin had brought her mount alongside Nessa.

'Keep away!' she warned, pointing the skelt blade towards me. 'Our trade is over, little mage, and you are no longer safe!'

'*You* claimed to be one who kept to her word!' I retorted angrily.

'I *did* keep my word!' the witch insisted. 'Did I not keep my promise and help you to slay the Haggenbrood? And once we left your abominable city, I did nothing to impede what you consider to be your lawful business.'

'You just play with words!' I shouted. 'I told you that I intended to sell Nessa in the slave market, as was my right. She was my chattel. And you replied that you would not hinder me in that.'

'You sold a slave in Karpotha and thus discharged your duties under the law of Bindos. That is what is truly important. The fact that I was that slave matters nought. It was done and, with our trade completed, I was free to liberate the slaves from the kulad. And know this and remember it well: I cannot allow your people to continue to hold human slaves!

'I declare war on the Kobalos. I go to forge the Star Blade, but once my business with this is done,' she cried, holding up the sack, 'I will return with my sisters and we will pull down the walls of Valkarky and kill all the Kobalos within! So remain at your haizda, mage! Keep away from that cursed city and you might live a little while longer! But now, lest we fight to the death prematurely, I would ask you a question. Why did you return to Karpotha and witness what I had done?'

'I returned to the cliff and sheltered from the storm,' I answered.

'That necessitated your delay but you did not need to return to the kulad. I know why you went back. You intended to buy Nessa's freedom. Is that not so?'

I was shocked by Grimalkin's words. How could she know this?

I nodded.

She smiled. 'So in that case, what has been lost? Nessa has the freedom you intended for her and it has been achieved at no financial or legal cost to yourself. Now I will return some of these women to their own lands. Others, even if born in the skleech pens, will be found homes amongst humans. As for Nessa, I will reunite her with her sister. In the meantime you will go home and prosper. You are looking forward to returning to your haizda – is that not true?'

I nodded again; then, finally finding my voice, I lifted my sabre and pointed it towards her. 'One day there will be a reckoning between us – I promise you that!'

'And I return that promise, so go in peace, Slither. One day we will surely meet again, but there is no need for us to spill more blood this day. I will go and attend to my own business. In the meantime, ready yourself for my return. Gather your resources, hone your fighting skills and strengthen your magic. Then we will meet and fight to the death, thus proving once and for all which of us is the stronger. I will take great pleasure in defeating such a formidable warrior. Is it a trade?'

'Yes! It is a trade!' I cried, lifting my sabre in salute.

Her words were wise. My magic was gone and must be replenished with blood. Better to face her when I was once again at the height of my powers. I looked forward to it.

She smiled, showing her pointed teeth, then rode her horse back to the head of the column.

Nessa remained where she was. 'Is that true? Did you really intend to buy me back and give me my freedom?' she asked.

'It is true, little Nessa. Grimalkin does not lie, although I think she finds too much freedom within the terms of a trade. I am more concerned with the precise letter of the contract.'

Nessa smiled. 'But I think she kept closely to the spirit of the agreement. Is that not true?'

It took me almost a week to reach my haizda again. The journey was delayed somewhat because, on the evening of the third day, I suddenly grew exceedingly thirsty. So great and immediate was my need that I was forced to plunge my teeth into the neck of my horse and drain its blood.

Usually I am able to resist such impulses, but the long days and nights of restraint – when I had stopped myself from leaping on one of Nessa's plump sisters and drinking until she died – suddenly took their toll. After such prolonged discipline there must be release. It is only natural for a Kobalos.

Winter is approaching once more, and I am preparing for my customary hibernation. I have spent the short summer in my haizda, drinking blood, reaping souls, sharpening my skills as a warrior and strengthening my magic. Now the final stage of my preparations will take place as I sleep.

I will be ready for the return of the witch. Whatever the outcome, I look forward to combat with Grimalkin. It will mark the pinnacle of my endeavours as a warrior mage. She has threatened the city of Valkarky. Although there is little love between me and certain of its inhabitants, I have an allegiance to my own people.

Perhaps I will be the means to end that threat.

Slither

Each day the sun crosses the sky a little closer to the horizon; soon the short summer will draw to a close.

Now my uncle knows the full story of how Susan died and how I was carried off to be a slave. It made him angry but also fearful. He says that the world is cooling and it makes him apprehensive. He remembers the tales of his grandparents; ancient fearful stories passed down through the generations.

When Golgoth, the Lord of Winter, last awoke, the ice expanded and the Kobalos beasts travelled south with it, slaying the men and boys but sparing the women and their daughters and carrying them off to be slaves. My uncle believes that it will happen again; but he prays that it will not be in his lifetime.

My aunt and uncle are good-hearted and have given shelter to Bryony and me; this is my home now. We work hard, but I also worked hard on Father's farm. Little has changed in that respect.

The time since my poor father's death has been terrifying and traumatic, but it has opened my eyes to just how big the world is and shown me that there are so many unknowns, so many new things to learn.

In a way that has made me restless and discontented with the routines of life. I would like to travel and see more of the world.

Maybe I have not seen the last of Grimalkin or of Slither. It is just a hunch, but I believe that one day our paths will cross again. I hope so . . .

Nessa

Slither's Dream

Little Nessa beckons me
By tapping on her silken knee.
She's trapped behind a prison grille
So I think to bend it to my will.
That iron grille is tall and wide
And spans the room from side to side
From floor to ceiling and wall to wall,
And though at present I am not tall,
My haizda magic's very strong;
It coils and twists and flicks the grille
Until the metal quivers, twists and yields
Like poppies dancing in the fields –
For that grille's alive, no doubt of that;
It's lithe and stretchy like a cat.
Now it opens very wide
And I beckon Nessa to my side.
As we climb the twisty tunnel stairs,
Nessa holds my hand and purrs,
But a shadow begins to grow and coil

Like a serpent slick with poisonous oil,
Like the withering breath of a daemon lord
Or a thing un-blest that raps on boards.
But my silver blade is very sharp,
It weaves strange patterns in the dark.
Its curvy point is sharp and long
More thirsty than my slithery tongue.
A fainter heart might here have prayed,
But I stand my ground
And draws my blade!
One shatek screaming in the night
Has startled armies into flight,
For a shatek's brood share a single soul
Taking many forms with a single goal,
And its whole's a creature called a djinn
An entity that's spawned to spin
A web of darkness round the sun
And puncture with a probing pin
All pleasures that be clothed with skin;
It's nursed its envy in the dark
And clothed its hope with a leprous bark
Like the dark Jibberdee of Old Combesarke!
And little Nessa it did see
And carried her off against her will
To imprison her behind that grille.
By that it aimed to summon me
To a final battle 'neath its tree.
For above this pit a great tree stands

That casts a shadow across the land;
It grows above the shatek's lair
At the very top of the thousandth stair
And bears fruit of such slimy green
That would taint the womb of a virgin queen.
Its leaves they twist and turn and glower
And fall each spring in a malevolent shower
To poison soul and wither breast
And churn the soil so the dead can't rest.
But my silver blade is very sharp,
It weaves strange patterns in the dark.
Its curvy point is sharp and long,
As thirsty as my slithery tongue.
So I wield my blade
And my blade's my song!
Six feet begin to tap on stone
With a click and a snap of flexing bone,
As with agile flesh and cunning leers
They seek to multiply my fears.
But I whirl my blade with a swish and hiss
Because I've been there and I've done this;
I've seen the sand that hides the stains,
I've seen the corpses bound with chains,
I've seen the daemon lord called 'Hob',
And I've heard the falling virgins sob.
For I know the pit where his mother lies,
Smelled the blood, heard the drone of flies,
Seen the vultures haunt the skies.

And I know this dance,
I know its pattern well,
Even better than the path to Hell!
So I lift my blade and licks my lips
Until six eyes pop like orange pips
And I shuffles left and I shuffles right
And weaves strange patterns in the night.
First blood to me as I takes a head
With a blow so swift it out-speeds dread,
Then quick as thought I strikes again,
And two heads roll now as a pair,
And squelch and bounce from stair to stair
Deep down in the bowels of the shatek's lair.
O boastful lord of this ancient tree,
What a fool you be to mess with me!
For I've tortured sharks in the deepest seas
And made them vomit boggarts' knees;
I've savaged eagles in their nests
And bit the bones from ogres' chests;
I've hunted vampires in the east
And laughed in the face of Satan's priest.
O boastful lord of this ancient tree,
This is what Nessa swore to me:
That our love was like a petal tree,
And ere the sun falls in the sea
I've promised Nessa she'll be free!
But he tries once more to cut me down
With a twist, a leer and an evil frown.

But I shuffle left and I shuffle right,
And strike a blow with all my might.
And through helmet, hauberk, shield and breast,
My blade it cuts from east to west.
Faster than falcon stoops to prey
My blade it cuts that fiend away.
O boastful lord of this ancient tree,
What a fool you were to mess with me,
For even in death I'm bound to win
Despite my darkest secret sin,
For I'll go to a world called Kinderquest,
A sphere where even the damned are blest.
Where they can rest for a thousand years
In a deep warm sleep beyond all fears,
Until when bored with 'safe and dark'
They spread new wings and soar with the lark
High into a heaven of the deepest blue
Where all their secret dreams come true.
The battle's over, the victory's won
But the final deed is not yet done.
For little Nessa I do see
Still tapping on her silken knee!
So I carve her flesh in succulent slices
And add a pinch of pungent spices.
Then boil her up to make a broth
And soothe away my latent wrath.
For although I loved our downy bed
I'm happier still when I've been fed!

An Extract from the Notebooks of Nicholas Browne, a Spook from Ancient Times

GLOSSARY OF THE KOBALOS WORLD

Anchiette: A burrowing mammal found in northern forests on the edge of the snow-line. The Kobalos consider them a delicacy eaten raw. There is little meat on the creature, but the leg bones are chewed with relish.

Askana: This is the dwelling place of the Kobalos gods. Probably just another term for the dark.

Baelic: The ordinary low tongue of the Kobalos people, used only in informal situations between family or to show friendship. The true language of the Kobalos is Losta, which is also spoken by humans who border their territory. For a stranger to speak to another Kobalos in Baelic implies warmth, but it is sometimes used before a 'trade' is made.

Balkai: The first and most powerful of the three Kobalos High Mages who formed the Triumvirate after the slaying of the king and now rule Valkarky.

Berserkers: These are Kobalos warriors sworn to die in battle.

Boska: This is the breath of a Kobalos mage which can be used to induce sudden unconsciousness, paralysis or terror within a human victim. The mage varies the effects of boska by altering the chemical composition of his breath. It is also sometimes used to change the mood of animals.

Bindos: Bindos is the Kobalos law that demands each citizen sell at least one purra in the slave markets every forty years. Failure to do so makes the perpetrator of the crime an outcast, shunned by his fellows.

Bychon: This is the Kobalos name for the spirit known in the County as a boggart.

Chaal: A substance used by a haizda mage to control the responses of his human victim.

Cougis: Dog-headed god whose red star can be seen in the sky.

Cumular Mountains: A high mountain range that marks the northwestern boundary of the Southern Peninsula.

Dendar Mountains: The high mountain range about seventy leagues southwest of Valkarky. In its foothills is the large kulad known as Karpotha. More slaves are bought and sold here than in all the other fortresses put together.

Dexturai: Kobalos changelings which are born of human females. Such creatures, although totally human in appearance, are easily susceptible to the will of any Kobalos. They are extremely strong and hardy and have the ability to become great warriors.

Eblis: This is the foremost of the Shaiksa, the Kobalos Brotherhood of assassins. He slew the last King of Valkarky using a magical lance called the Kangadon. It is believed that he is over two thousand years old and it is certain that he has never been bested in combat. The Brotherhood refer to him by two other designations: He Who Cannot Be Defeated and He Who Can Never Die.

Erestaba: The Plain of Erestaba lies just north of the Shanna River within the territory of the Kobalos.

Fittzanda Fissure: This is also known as the Great Fissure. It is an area of earthquakes and instability that marks the southern boundary of the Kobalos territories.

Galena Sea: The sea southeast of Combesarke. It lies between that kingdom and Pennade.

Gannar Glacier: The great ice-flow whose source is the Cumular Mountains.

Ghanbalsam: A resinous material bled from a ghanbala tree by a haizda mage and used as a base for ointments such as chaal.

Ghanbala: The deciduous gum tree most favoured as a dwelling by a Kobalos haizda mage.

Haggenbrood: A warrior entity bred from the flesh of a human female. Its function is one of ritual combat. It has three selves which share a common mind; they are, to all intents and purposes, one creature.

Haizda: This is the territory of a haizda mage; here he hunts and farms the human beings he owns. He takes blood from them, and occasionally their souls.

Haizda mage: A rare type of Kobalos mage who dwells in his own territory far from Valkarky and gathers wisdom from territory he has marked as his own.

Homunculus: A small creature bred from the purrai in the skleech pens. They often have several selves which, like the Haggenbrood, are controlled by a single mind. However, rather than being identical, each self has a specialized function and only one of them is capable of speaking Losta.

Hubris: The sin of pride against the gods. The full wrath of the gods is likely to be directed against one who persists in this sin in the face of repeated warnings. The very act of becoming a mage is in itself an act of hubris, and few live to progress beyond the period of noviciate.

Hybuski: Hybuski (commonly known as hyb) are a special type of warrior created and employed in battle by the Kobalos. They are a hybrid of Kobalos and horse, but possess other attributes designed for combat. Their upper body is hairy and muscular, combining exceptional strength with speed. They are capable of ripping an opponent to pieces. Their hands are also specially adapted for fighting.

Kangadon: This is the Lance That Cannot Be Broken, also known as the King Slayer, a lance of power crafted by the Kobalos High Mages – although some believe that it was forged by their blacksmith god, Olkie.

Karpotha: The kulad in the foothills of the Dendar Mountains which holds the largest purrai slave markets. Most are held early in the spring.

Kashilowa: The gatekeeper of Valkarky, which is responsible for either allowing or refusing admittance to the city. It is a huge creature with one thousand legs and was created by mage magic to carry out its function.

Kastarand: This is the word for the Kobalos' Holy War. They will wage it to rid the land of the humans, whom they believe to be the descendants of escaped slaves. It cannot begin until Talkus, the god of the Kobalos, is born.

Kirrhos: This is the 'tawny death' that comes to victims of the Haggenbrood.

Kulad: A defensive tower built by the Kobalos that marks strategic positions on the border of their territories. Others deeper within their territory are used as slave markets.

League: The distance a galloping horse can cover in five minutes.

Lenklewth: The second of the three Kobalos High Mages who form the Triumvirate.

Losta: This is the language spoken by all who inhabit the Southern Peninsula. This includes the Kobalos, who claim that the language was stolen and degraded by mankind. The Kobalos version of Losta contains a lexis almost one third larger than that used by humans, and perhaps gives some credence to their claims. It is certainly a linguistic anomaly that two distinct species should share a common language.

Mages: There are many types of human mage; the same is also true of the Kobalos. But for an outsider they are difficult to describe and categorize. However, the highest rank is nominally that of a High Mage. There is also one type, the haizda mage, that does not fit within that hierarchy, for these are outsiders who dwell in their own individual territories far from Valkarky. Their powers are hard to quantify.

Mandrake: Sometimes called mandragora, this is a root that resembles the human form and is sometimes used by a Kobalos mage to give focus to the power that dwells within his mind.

Meljann: The third of three Kobalos High Mages who form the Triumvirate.

Northern Kingdoms: This is the collective name sometimes given to the small kingdoms, such as Pwodente and Wayaland, which lie south of the Great Fissure. More usually it refers to all the kingdoms north of Shallotte and Serwentia.

Noviciate: This is the first stage of the learning process undertaken by a haizda mage, which lasts approximately thirty years. The candidate studies under one of the older and most powerful mages. If the noviciate is completed satisfactorily, the mage must then go off alone to study and develop his craft.

Oscher: A substance which can be used as emergency food for horses; made from oats, it has special chemical additives that can sustain a beast of burden for the duration of a long journey. Unfortunately it results in a severe shortening of the animal's life.

Olkie: This is the god of Kobalos blacksmiths. He has four arms, and teeth made of brass. It is believed that he crafted the Kangadon, the magical lance that cannot be deflected from its target.

Oussa: The elite guard that serves and defends the Triumvirate; also used to guard parties of slaves taken from Valkarky to the kulads to be bought and sold.

Triumvirate: The ruling body of Valkarky, composed of the three most powerful High Mages in the city. It was first formed after the King of Valkarky was slain by Eblis, the Shaiksa assassin. It is essentially a dictatorship that uses ruthless means to hold onto power. Others are always waiting in the wings to replace the three mages.

Plunder Room: This is the vault where the Triumvirate store the items they have confiscated either by the power of magic, force of arms or legal process. It is the most secure place in Valkarky.

Purra (pl. purrai): The term used to denote one of the female pure-bred stock of humans bred into slavery by the Kobalos. The term is also applicable to those females who dwell within a haizda.

Salamander: A fire dragon tulpa.

Shaiksa: This is the highest order of Kobalos assassins. If one is slain, the remainder of the Brotherhood are honour-bound to hunt down his killer.

Shakamure: The magecraft of haizda mages which draws its power from the taking of human blood and the borrowing of souls.

Shanna River: The Shanna marks the old border between the northern human kingdoms and the territory of the Kobalos. Now Kobalos are often to be found south of this line. The treaty that agreed this border has long been disregarded by both sides.

Shatek (also known as a djinn): This is a warrior entity with three selves and a single controlling mind. It differs from the Haggenbrood in that it was created to be deployed in battle. A number of them have rebelled and are no longer subject to Kobalos authority. They dwell far from Valkarky bringing death and terror to the lands surrounding their lairs.

Shudru: The Kobalos term for the harsh winter of the Northern Kingdoms.

Skaiium: A time when a haizda mage faces a dangerous softening of his predatory nature.

Skapien: A small secret group of Kobalos within Valkarky who are opposed to the trade in purrai.

Skelt: This is a creature that lives near water and kills its victims by inserting its long snout into their bodies and draining their blood. The Kobalos believe it is the shape that their god, Talkus, will assume at his birth.

Skleech pens: Pens within Valkarky where the Kobalos keep human female slaves, using them for food or to breed other new species and hybrid forms to do their bidding.

Sklutch: This is a type of creature employed by the Kobalos as servants. Its speciality is cleaning the rapidly growing fungus from the walls and ceilings of the dwellings within Valkarky.

Skoya: The material formed within the bodies of the whoskor of which Valkarky is constructed.

Skulka: A poisonous water snake whose bite induces instant paralysis. It is much favoured by Kobalos assassins, who use it to render their victims helpless before slaying them. After death, its toxins are impossible to detect in the victim's blood.

Slarinda: These are the females of the Kobalos. They have been extinct for over three thousand years. They were murdered – slain by a cult of Kobalos males who hated women. Now Kobalos males are born of purrai, human females held prisoner in the skleech pens.

Talkus: The god of the Kobalos who is not yet born. In form he will resemble the creature known as a *skelt*. Talkus means the God Who Is Yet to Be. He is sometimes also referred to as the Unborn.

Therskold: A threshold upon which a word of interdiction or harming has been laid. This is a potent area of haizda strength and it is dangerous – even for a human mage – to cross such a portal.

Trade: Although the unit of currency is the *valcron*, many Kobalos, particularly haizda mages, rely on what they call 'trade'. This implies an exchange of goods or services, but it is much more than that. It is a question of honour, and each party must keep its word even if to do so means death.

Tulpa: A creature created within the mind of a mage and occasionally given form in the outer world.

Ulska: A deadly but rare Kobalos poison that burns its victim from within. It is also excreted from glands at the base of the claws of the Haggenbrood. It results in kirrhos, which is known as the 'tawny death'.

Unktus: A minor Kobalos deity worshipped only by the lowest menials of the city. He is depicted with very small horns curving backwards from the crown of his head.

Valkarky: The chief city of the Kobalos, which lies just within the Arctic Circle. Valkarky means the City of the Petrified Tree.

Valcron: A small coin, often referred to as a *valc*, accepted throughout the Southern Peninsula. Made of an alloy which

is one tenth silver, a valcron is the wage paid daily to a
Kobalos foot soldier.

Whalakai: Known as a vision of what is, this is an instant of
perception that comes to either a High Mage or a haizda
mage. It is an epiphany, a moment of revelation, when the
totality of a situation, with all the complexities that have led
to it, are known to him in a flash of insight. The Kobalos
believe this is a vision given to the mage by Talkus, their God
Who Is Yet to Be, its purpose being to facilitate the path to his
birth.

Whoskor: The collective name for the creatures subservient to
the Kobalos who are engaged in the never-ending task of
extending the city of Valkarky. They have sixteen legs, eight
of which also function as arms, and are used to shape the
skoya, the soft stone which they exude from their mouths.

Widdershins: A movement that is anti-clockwise or against the
sun. Seen as counter to the natural order of things, it is sometimes employed by a Kobalos mage to assert his will upon
the cosmos. Filled with hubris, it holds within it great risk.

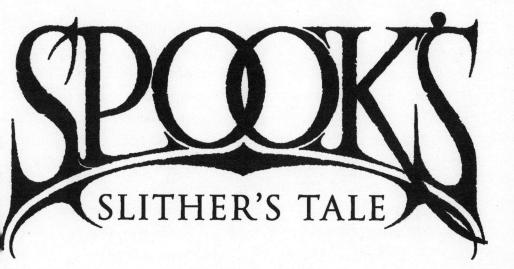

Joseph Delaney is a retired English teacher living in
Lancashire. He has three children and nine grandchildren,
and often speaks at conference, library and bookshop events.
His home is in the middle of Boggart territory and his
village has a boggart called the Hall Knocker, which was
laid to rest under the step of a house near the church.

Most of the places in the Spook's books are based on
real places in Lancashire, and the inspiration behind the
stories often comes from local ghost stories and legends.

You can visit the Wardstone Chronicles website at
www.**spooksbooks**.com
where you can find Joseph's blog
and more information on the books.

Turn over now to read some of Joseph's thoughts
on his bestselling series . . .

Hear what Joseph has to say about the forthcoming Spook's film, *The Seventh Son* . . .

Slither's Tale takes us a long way away from the County, and Tom and the Spook do not appear in the story. What made you want to write such a different kind of Wardstone Chronicles book?

I like to try new things and it was fun to write about a totally new place with new characters. However, sometimes characters take over! Grimalkin forced her way into the book and plays a significant part, making Slither very much a part of the Wardstone Chronicles series!

✛

The book introduces us to many new places and lots of new creatures. How do you come up with the different names for them?

I keep a notebook and arrive at their names by trial and error with the occasional moment of sudden inspiration. There are so many new creatures in this book that I decided to include a glossary. Who knows, maybe at some point all this will be incorporated into an extended Spook's Bestiary!

✛

Which characters in the Spook's series do you most enjoy writing for?

I enjoy writing for Tom, Alice and the Spook but at the moment Grimalkin is my favourite.

Your books are so scary that every copy comes with the warning that they are 'not to be read after dark!' Which writers or books have terrified you into sleeping with one light on?

No books or writers have ever done that to me – yet! However, as child I slept with a candle (the old terraced house we lived in didn't even have electricity at first) because of my nightmares!

✦

Will there be more books about Slither and the world of the Kobalos?

Yes, I am confident that Slither will return. Between Grimalkin and the Kobalos there is much unfinished business! Maybe next time the story could be told from her point of view. Who knows – Tom might even go with her! We shall see.

✦

It's recently been announced that *The Spook's Apprentice* is being turned into a film, *The Seventh Son.* Are you excited to see your work brought to the silver screen?

Yes, I am very excited and look forward to seeing it when it happens! However, each person who reads a book has an internal imaginative film-show generated by the words on the page. The silver screen can never match that, which is why some readers are disappointed by the film interpretation of a favourite book. But I am optimistic! When I visited the film set in Vancouver I saw Jeff Bridges in action and he is a very convincing Spook!

✛

Is it difficult to let go of your creation to a film company? Do you feel like you want to be on set directing it all yourself, or are you intrigued to see their take on it?

I think you have to let go and have faith that they will produce a great film. Being a writer is my favourite job but my second choice would to be a film director! I am very intrigued to see their adaptation of *The Spook's Apprentice.* There will be differences from the book but I really believe that it will be good entertainment and a great commercial success.

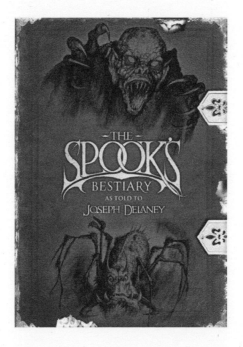

THE SPOOK'S BESTIARY

AS TOLD TO JOSEPH DELANEY

Dear finder of this book,
What you hold in your hands is my BESTIARY – my personal account of
the denizens of the dark I've encountered, together with the lessons I have
learned, and the mistakes I have made. I have held nothing back . . .
By possessing this book I am counting on you to continue my battle
against the dark. Do not let me down.
Yours,
John Gregory

A complete guide and companion to Joseph Delaney's
phenomenally successful Spook's stories, this fascinating,
lavishly illustrated Bestiary is a replica of the Spook's own
notebook; John Gregory's life's work and findings.

'The illustrations . . . are stunning. It is a brooding and eerie
collection of stories for reading in one sitting or dipping into.'
Jake Hope – *The Bookseller*

ISBN: 978 0 370 32979 6

Meet Grimalkin again . . .

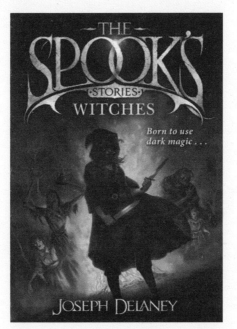

THE SPOOK'S STORIES: WITCHES

BY JOSEPH DELANEY

Born to use dark magic . . .

Read five dark and terrifying witch stories from the Spook's own collection. There are child-eating witches, witch assassins, Celtic witches, dead witches, and witches so beautiful they can break a man's heart.

These stories will chill your blood and frighten you to your very bones. Just remember not to read them after dark.

'This to me was a refresher of all things good in the Joseph Delaney world . . . This is a great book to read, it will entice you to read all of the books in the series from start to finish'

Mr Ripley's Enchanted Books

ISBN: 978 1 862 30987 6

If you have dared to enter the world of the Spook,
you might like these other books published
by Random House Children's Publishers UK. . .

Read them if you dare . . .

SERAPHINA
BY RACHEL HARTMAN

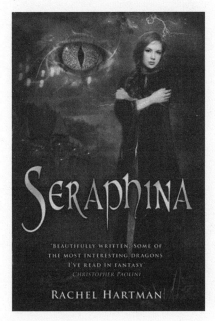

A fragile peace has been achieved in the realm of Goredd, and dragons
and humans live together in harmony.

But the truce is shattered when a royal prince is brutally murdered –
could dragons be to blame?

Seraphina, a talented court musician harbouring secrets of her own,
is drawn into the investigation and uncovers a darker plot, one that
threatens the very existence of the kingdom. And soon her own life
is in terrible danger as she fights to hide the secret behind her
amazing gift . . .

'Beautifully written. Some of the most interesting dragons I've read in
fantasy' *Christopher Paolini*

ISBN: 978 0 857 53156 8

BROTHERBAND: THE OUTCASTS

BY JOHN FLANAGAN

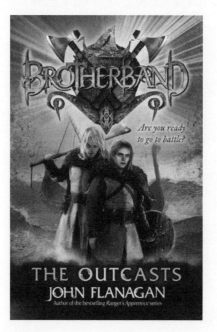

There is only one way to become a warrior.

Boys are chosen for teams called Brotherbands and must endure
months of gruelling battles in the treacherous sea. Hal finds
himself the unwilling leader of a band of outcasts, the boys that no
one wants. They are small and wiry but what they lack in size, they
make up with skill and courage. Now they must battle against the
other bands in the ultimate race where there can only be one winner.

The icy waters make the sea a dangerous playing field.
Especially when – for some – this is *anything* but a game . . .

ISBN: 978 0 440 86992 4

THE SECRETS OF THE IMMORTAL
NICHOLAS FLAMEL: THE ALCHEMYST
BY MICHAEL SCOTT

He holds the secret that can end the world.

The truth: Nicholas Flamel was born in Paris on 28 September 1330.
Nearly seven hundred years later, he is acknowledged as the greatest
Alchemyst of his day. It is said that he discovered the secret of eternal life.

The records show that he died in 1418. But his tomb is empty.

The legend: Nicholas Flamel lives. But only because he has been
making the elixir of life for centuries. The secret of eternal life is hidden
within the powerful book he protects – the Book of Abraham the Mage.
In the wrong hands, it will destroy the world.

That's exactly what Dr John Dee plans to do when he steals it.
Humankind won't know what's happening until it's too late.
And if the prophecy is right, Sophie and Josh Newman are
the only ones with the power to save the world as we know it.

Sometimes legends are true.

And Sophie and Josh Newman are about to find themselves
in the middle of the greatest legend of all time.

ISBN: 978 0 552 56252 2

THE PALADIN PROPHECY
BY MARK FROST

There is only one way to become a warrior.
Will West is careful to live life under the radar. At his parents' insistence,
he's made sure to get mediocre grades and to stay in the middle of the
pack on his cross-country team. Then Will slips up, accidentally scoring
off the charts on a nationwide exam, and he is recruited by an exclusive
and mysterious prep school – the best school no one's ever heard of,
with technology the likes of which no one's ever seen.

At the same time, coincidentally – or not so – Will realizes he's being
followed by men in dark hats, driving black sedans who pose a terrifying threat to his family. What follows is a series of events and revela-
tions that places Will smack in the middle of a millennia old struggle
between titanic forces . . .

ISBN: 978 0 857 53120 9